GUNMAN'S ODDS

Other Avalon Books by Clifford Blair

BROTHERHOOD OF WARRIORS
DEVIL'S CANYON DOUBLE CROSS

GUNMAN'S ODDS

Clifford Blair

AVALON BOOKS
THOMAS BOUREGY AND COMPANY, INC.
401 LAFAYETTE STREET
NEW YORK, NEW YORK 10003

JH DM BA JM

PRINTED IN THE UNITED STATES OF AMERICA
BY HADDON CRAFTSMEN, SCRANTON, PENNSYLVANIA

With love to my father
Dr. Clifford J. Blair
outstanding role model, adviser, and friend

Prologue

S cott Colton saw the five riders bearing down on their human prey, and he felt a quick ripping of anger. The victim was afoot and clad only in buckskin leggings. The early fall sun glinted from his copper-colored skin as he staggered in front of his pursuers. He was an Indian.

Scott put heels hard to the sides of his big sorrel mare. She carried him down the grassy slope of the hill at a gallop. The wind felt harsh and dry on his face.

The excited cries and shouts of the riders reached his ears clearly. They were keeping their horses to a lope, making no real effort to outdistance their faltering victim. They were making a cruel and savage game of it.

The lead rider added a new tactic. His arm snapped back and then forward. Scott glimpsed a peculiarly bent piece of wood go spinning end over end from his hand. It began to flatten out in its flight only an instant before it caught the running Indian square between the shoulder blades.

1

There was a strong force behind the strange object, and the Indian was knocked tumbling forward. He sprawled, then scrambled dazedly to his knees while the riders surrounded him. The man who had thrown the weapon leaned far from his saddle in a trick rider's maneuver to retrieve it.

Then the drumming of the sorrel's hooves pulled the group's attention to Scott. He slowed the mare as he approached. The Indian wore nothing in his hair or on his person to distinguish him as a member of any particular tribe. Many tribes had been forced to relocate here to Oklahoma Territory, and the brave could have come from any one of them.

With the recent opening of the Territory in the '89 land run, the Indians now shared an uneasy existence with the steadily growing population of whites that had flooded the region. After the dissolving of the reservation system and the opening of the Indian lands to settlement, the Indians had supposedly been elevated to equal status with the whites. Unfortunately, centuries of bigotry died hard, and such examples of persecution as Scott now witnessed were not infrequent.

The Indian was in early manhood, not much younger than Scott. He was big and muscular and had the proud bearing that spoke of a warrior's heritage. Perhaps it was a longing to experience a taste of that past tradition that had driven him out alone to stalk the prairie for game. Whatever his reasons for leaving the relative security of his village, he had now fallen victim to this vicious pack of riders. If Scott was any judge, the Indian might well pay for his hunting trip with his life.

The five riders all bore the unmistakable stamp of

hired guns, men who lived by their wits on the edge of the law and frequently beyond. They had shifted about to present a united front at Scott's approach. Strangers were always enemies to their breed until proven otherwise. Their hands hovered near their weapons, though with their numbers, they probably felt they had little to fear.

Scott pulled the sorrel to a halt some fifteen feet from them. With a grim sickness he realized that they recognized him as one of their own kind. They saw in him their own stamp of lawlessness. Would he ever be rid of it? he wondered. Or had his past marked his face and stance and soul irrevocably? It was not a pleasing thought, but just now that very bearing might give him an edge.

"You want in on this?"

The speaker was the lean, pale man who had used the peculiar throwing club to fell the Indian. He sat his horse with an insolent ease that showed itself also in the half sneer on his thin lips. His empty eyes were only a shade darker than his pale, sun-reddened skin.

He hefted the club easily in one hand, as if hoping for another excuse to use it. The weapon was a thin, flat piece of wood less than two feet in length, bent at about a forty-five-degree angle, and it did not appear to be heavy.

"He asked you a question, mister."

Scott shifted his eyes to the new speaker. Black haired and stunningly handsome, the big man was dressed in a tailored whipcord suit that must have been suffocatingly hot. But no trace of discomfort showed on his dark, rugged face. Scott thought that he would have looked more at home in the boardroom of a bank than out here on the plains, leading a pack of hardcases. And he was undoubtedly the leader of this hard crew. Their obsequious manner toward him bespoke that fact clearly.

"Well, mister, are you in or out?" the leader prodded.

"What is it I'd be getting into?" Scott kept his voice mild.

The leader smiled. It made his good looks disappear in an instant. His smile, Scott thought, was that of a demon. "Why, we're just doing a little hunting here. Big-game hunting, I guess you'd say." His tones were those of an educated man. His evil smile widened. "And we've got our prey run to ground."

Scott looked past him. The Indian had risen to his feet, and, panting, he watched the proceedings warily. No sign of fear showed in his dark eyes or on his broad face. At the slight movement of the leader's hand, the riders began to shift their mounts sideways. In moments, Scott realized, they would have him neatly bracketed. He could not afford to let them get clear of his field of fire.

"Hunt's over," Scott said, and drew his gun.

He made his movement as casual as that of the leader had been. It caught the gun crew by surprise. The sound of his thumbing back the hammer locked them in their places.

The smile vanished from the face of the leader. A scowl of anger replaced it, dark and bitter. It made his features almost as ugly as the smile.

"That's a fool move." Repressed savagery was in the

leader's words. "What do you think you can do against five of us?"

"This," Scott said. He shifted the gun and fired.

The .45 slug took the man at the right end of the line square in the shoulder. It twisted him almost out of the saddle. His gun fell from his spasmed hand. He had been drawing it under the distraction of the leader's words.

Scott swept the gun back to bear on the lean man. "Drop your toy!" he barked.

The man froze in the act of lifting his peculiar wooden club. His cruel eyes were fixed on Scott's face. Reluctantly he let the weapon fall. Scott tried to watch all of them at once. He had a vague impression of the Indian watching silently. He had not attempted to flee.

"We can kill you," the leader said lightly. He had regained his urbane equanimity and seemed almost amused at the turn of events.

"Maybe," Scott answered him. "But I can kill you too, and probably a few others as well."

"You're running against high odds for the sake of a mangy redskin."

"I just didn't see as how he needs killing," Scott explained. "Now, as to some of you boys, I can't say the same thing." The leader was right, Scott knew, in his evaluation of the odds. He was playing a dangerous game with this crew. One gun against four and maybe five. High odds for sure. And the stalemate could not hold indefinitely. But there was no regret in him.

"What's your name, kid?" the leader asked.

"Scott Colton."

The dark eyes blinked in the handsome face. "Bounty man, isn't it? From up north."

"That's right."

"Well, now, maybe the odds aren't as high as I thought." He inclined his head quizzically. "What brings you down here to these parts?"

Running from ghosts, Scott thought. "That any concern of yours?" he said.

The leader shrugged. "Could be." He seemed genuinely interested in Scott's replies. "I'm Land Talbot. Could be I'd have some use for a man like you."

A man like him, Scott thought bitterly. A bounty hunter and gunman with a rep that reached all the way down into the Territory. Was that what he had bought with the first twenty-five years of his life? "I'm retired," he said.

Talbot snorted in derisive amusement. "Sure you are. Men like us never retire willingly. It's a bullet or a rope that retires us."

"I'm not like you." Scott felt his teeth grind together. "Remember that."

Talbot's face sobered. "Sure, I'll remember it. And you remember something too. You've crossed me once now and come off light. I'll charge that to professional courtesy. But I've offered you a place with me. Think hard before you say no. People in these parts generally don't have the chance to turn me down twice."

"I just have," Scott told him coldly. "The answer's still no."

Talbot's face grew ugly. He was not smiling. "We'll see," he promised. "There are other days than this one.

Come on, boys." He hauled his big Appaloosa stallion around.

His pack of human predators followed suit. The lean gunman performed his acrobatic trick again to retrieve his throwing stick. He backed his horse expertly in the wake of the others. His eyes glowed harshly in his bloodless face. Then he lifted the curved club in a mocking salute. Pivoting his horse, he spurred after the others. The Indian had to sidestep to avoid the deliberate swerve of his horse.

Scott watched them go. He half expected them to turn back in a charge, or to unlimber their saddle guns and open fire. But their pace did not slow from a gallop as they raced across the rolling grassland.

Talbot's figure was still easily visible at their head— a big man on a big horse. He did not look back. The wounded man slumped precariously in his saddle. Scott found himself hoping that the man made it. He had no time to examine the strangeness of the thought.

He realized his palm was sweaty against the butt of his .45. Carefully he lowered the hammer, and quite automatically his fingers ejected the spent case from the cylinder and replaced it with a fresh cartridge from his belt. Despite his protests to the contrary, he still had the ingrained habits of a gunman, he reflected sourly. Except one, he amended the thought. When he had had the chance, he had shot to wound and not to kill.

He became aware of the Indian's steady gaze. He holstered the .45.

"Me Hunting Wolf." The Indian touched his burnished, muscular chest to confirm his introduction.

"Scott Colton," Scott responded.

Hunting Wolf nodded solemnly. "I and my people will remember name of Scott Colton. Today you save my life. Tomorrow my life is yours."

"Are your people close to here?" Scott asked.

A gaunt, sinewy arm swept to the west. "Some miles there. I hunting. Lose my bow when white men attack me."

A bow instead of a gun. He had been right about the purpose of the hunting trip, Scott thought. He nodded after the riders. "Who are they?"

"White men from camp."

Scott frowned at the answer. "What camp?"

Another sweep of the arm, this time to the northeast, in the direction Talbot and his men had taken. "Big camp of white men in hills, some miles there."

An outlaw camp? Scott wondered. The presence of such an enclave would hardly be surprising, given the lawlessness of the Territory. "Does this kind of thing happen often?"

"Only when they catch my people alone." Hunting Wolf's voice was expressionless.

Scott shook his head grimly. He was not sure what to say. He felt responsible in some obscure way for the actions of Land Talbot and his men against Hunting Wolf's people.

"I go now," Hunting Wolf said. "You come? My people welcome you."

Scott shook his head. "No, thanks. I'll be heading on." He wanted to ask if Hunting Wolf would be safe returning to his village, but it might be an insult to the brave.

Hunting Wolf did not dispute his decision. "White

man's town there." He pointed to the south. "Big city there." He pointed slightly more east.

The big city would probably be Guthrie, the territorial capital. The town most likely was Meridian. Judging by the chase that Hunting Wolf had given them, Talbot and his men had almost certainly come from the direction of the town.

Hunting Wolf gave his solemn nod again. "I not forget you, Scott Colton," he promised. In two strides he hit a smooth, ground-consuming lope.

For a moment Scott watched the lithe form moving easily away across the grassland. Then he urged the sorrel mare to the south.

Chapter One

The steady sound of hammering came to him from up ahead. Scott had heard it for some minutes now. The laborer, whoever he was, certainly seemed industrious. The rutted road now led through a broad strip of woodland bordering a meandering stream.

He guessed he was nearing Meridian, because the road showed signs of regular use. He had already encountered another traveler on it. The wind-chapped and sunburned farmer had been driving a wagon laden with supplies. He had gazed suspiciously as Scott edged the sorrel aside to let him go by. As Scott nodded, the farmer's face relaxed only slightly as he nodded in return. He had glanced back searchingly at Scott once they had passed.

Ahead of him now, the hammering stopped briefly and then resumed. Through the trees Scott caught a glimpse of a white wooden cross raised against the sky. He heeled the sorrel on around the bend and saw the structure at last.

A church was being built here, and the cross he had glimpsed must have been put in place as soon as the frame of the structure was completed. It clearly proclaimed the nature of the building. The church sat on a hill at the boundary of the woodland, and it was not far from the edge of town. The buildings and dirt streets of Meridian were visible in the shallow valley below.

The laborer was a sandy-haired youth. Intent on his task, he did not look around from his hammering as Scott approached. Scott studied him briefly. How old was the boy? Sixteen or so, at a guess. The thought brought a stab of regret. What had he been doing at sixteen? Practicing with guns, he recalled. Certainly he had not been working to build a church. He felt a fleeting envy for the young laborer and the opportunities that were open to him. They were opportunities that he himself, in one way or another, had long since lost.

The sorrel shied impatiently, and the boy spun about sharply, with surprise, anger, and maybe fear in his face. A Winchester saddle gun leaned against the wall beside him. Swiftly he reached for it.

"Hey!" Scott yelled at him. Its abruptness made the boy falter for a brief moment. "If I was your enemy, you'd already be dead," Scott told him.

Reluctantly the boy straightened. "I guess so," he admitted sullenly. His eyes darted toward the Winchester.

"Too late for that now," Scott advised. "When you go for a gun, don't hesitate. But I'll ride out if you're that set on gunplay." He knew he was stupid to turn his back on the boy, but he turned the sorrel just the same.

"Wait a minute, mister." The boy's voice carried an

apologetic tone, and Scott reined back around. "I'm sorry," the boy went on. "I thought you were somebody else, that's all."

Scott hesitated. Common sense told him to ride out, but the resignation and weariness in the boy's face made him stay where he was. "Fellow your age usually hasn't had time to make enough enemies so that he feels any need to throw down on every stranger that crosses his path," he commented. *I was the exception to that rule when I was a boy,* he added silently.

"They're my pa's enemies," the boy said. He paused a moment. "But I guess that makes them mine too."

Scott made his decision, and he swung down from the sorrel. The teen watched him carefully, but made no further move toward the Winchester. "Who's your pa?" Scott asked.

"Reverend Samuel Prentiss. He likes to go by Brother Sam."

A preacher man, Scott thought. He gestured at the half-finished structure. "Is this his church?"

The boy's face brightened. "It's going to be as soon as we get it finished." He turned away for a jug beside a pile of lumber. "If you're thirsty, I've got some water here." He picked up the jug to offer it.

"Thanks." Scott took the jug and drank. The water was still cool. He passed it back and the youth drank thirstily. Scott remembered the steady sound of hammering. The boy had been working hard.

"I'm Scott Colton." He offered his hand as the boy lowered the jug.

"Matthew Prentiss." His grip was firmer than Scott had expected.

"You go by Matt?"

"Yeah." He set the jug back down in the shade of the lumber.

Scott studied the church. "You and your pa do good work."

Matt's face was expressionless as he nodded. "Thanks."

Scott studied him. "Your pa's got enemies hereabouts?" he probed.

Matt shrugged and turned away. "Some folks don't like the idea of a church in these parts, I reckon."

Scott frowned. "Seems like most towns would welcome a preacher coming to start a church."

"That's what we thought." Matt gazed broodingly up at the church frame.

Scott gripped one of the boards of the structure. "Where's your pa now?" he asked without looking back at Matt.

"He and my sister are in town getting supplies. We're planning to move out here from the rent house where we've been staying."

"You expecting trouble?" Scott turned back to face him. What business of his was this, anyway? he wondered remotely. He'd had few dealings with churches or preachers in his life.

"Like I said, some folks don't like the idea of a church here," Matt answered him. "Pa felt the call to come to these parts and set up a church. We got this land here from a fellow fixing to move back East. We heard some talk in town about whether or not a church was needed here. Pa didn't pay it no mind. He's always said that the place where folks don't want a church is likely the place where they need it the most. Anyway, things was going fine until this morning."

"What happened?" Scott settled his shoulders against the boards of the framed building.

"Group of men came by. Told us we had no business here, and that if we didn't move out, they'd move us."

"What kind of men? Townspeople?"

Matt shook his head. "No, these weren't townspeople," he said grimly.

"Big, handsome man named Land Talbot and a crew of gunsels?" Scott guessed with sudden intuition.

Matt tensed. "How'd you know?" he demanded in quick, sharp suspicion.

"I ran into them a ways back out on the prairie," Scott explained casually.

Matt continued to study him intently.

"Relax, boy," Scott told him. "I ain't one of them."

Matt flushed and looked away. "I'm sorry. It's just that you look—I mean, I thought at first—" He broke off.

"Forget it," Scott advised. *I know,* he thought sourly. *It's just that I look like one of them.* "Where's your ma?" he asked to change the subject.

"She died a few years back," Matt said, making an effort not to show any unmanly emotion.

"That's rough." Scott regretted the question.

Matt shrugged. He looked back at the church frame. "I guess I'd better be getting back to work."

Scott felt a pang. He didn't want the conversation to end. The realization surprised him. He was not even sure why he had stopped to visit in the first place. It was usually not in his nature to be this open with strangers. He dismissed the thought. "Be seeing you," he said.

"Yeah." Matt was studying the church as if gauging a worthy opponent.

Another pang pierced Scott. He understood suddenly that he envied this boy his dedication to his task. Matt Prentiss, for all his youth, had a goal to which he was clearly committed. What did he himself have, Scott reflected, except the goal of freeing himself from the burdens of his past? He mounted the sorrel and laid the reins against her neck.

"Hey!" Matt's voice stopped him.

He turned the sorrel back. Matt had picked up his hammer. An afterthought seemed to have struck him. "If you're going to be in town for a few days, come to our service Sunday morning," he invited.

Scott nodded at the half-built structure. "You don't have a church yet," he pointed out.

"This is just a building." Matt gestured with the hammer. "We don't need it to have services. We'll just meet outdoors here. Pa will preach, and then there's a potluck dinner." Some of his sullenness had slipped away. The sincerity behind the offer was plain in his disarming grin.

When was the last time he had been invited to church? Scott wondered. "Thanks for the invite," he said. His voice sounded gruff in his own ears. He reined the sorrel around and drummed his heels against her ribs to move her out. Behind him he heard the hammering start again.

The sound faded as he rode on down toward the town. Meridian consisted mostly of frame buildings. It was a thriving community, boasting both a railway station and a stagecoach stop.

Part of the town's prosperity, Scott knew, resulted from its rather unsavory connection with the territorial capital of Guthrie, some eleven miles distant. Meridian's saloons, gambling halls, and pleasure palaces provided a discreet playground for the prominent businessmen of Guthrie. In their smaller sister community, the founding fathers of Guthrie could safely indulge their baser appetites without fear of embarrassment or public scandal.

Scott saw evidence of this dubious relationship in the bars and gaming houses lining the main street. Painted women—old in experience if not in years—watched him openly from bar windows and doorways as he rode past. It was too early yet for much activity, but a few cowhands and other customers were already patronizing the disreputable establishments.

Guthrie itself, the capital, was widely known as a rambunctious community. Scott guessed that this part of Meridian was no place for those weak at heart or strong of virtue. He grimaced. Perhaps Matt's father was right about the need of a church here.

He entered a more reputable stretch of Main Street and rode by a two-story frame bank. The upper floor appeared to serve as living quarters for the financial institution's proprietor and his family. Catty-cornered across the street from the bank was a long, one-story building with a sign proclaiming it a general store. A wagon was parked in front of it. Three burly hardcases lounged on the porch by the doorway. Beside the store was a stable.

The afternoon was well along, Scott reflected, and Guthrie was still a good piece distant, if he even wanted to go there. He had been too long without a roof to sleep under, and Meridian offered as good a stopping place as any other for a man whose only destination was somewhere away from his past.

When he reined in at the stable, the sorrel caught the scent of hay and feed and other horses, and she snorted in anticipation.

A gangly man, lantern-jawed and well up in years, sauntered out of the dark interior of the stable. He blinked at the bright sunlight and scanned the street first one way and then the other. He cocked up his head to regard Scott. "Howdy," he drawled.

Scott returned the greeting and dismounted.

The oldster snorted. "I was wondering if you wanted me to board your mare with you still sitting there on top of her."

Scott grinned. "Depends on how much a room and bath goes for around here."

The fellow took the sorrel's reins in a gnarled hand. Then he pointed across the way with his chin. "Rooming house yonder. They'll treat you right."

Scott nodded his thanks.

"You planning to board her here long?" Sharp eyes studied Scott from the leathery face.

"That depends too." Scott kept his tone agreeable. Once he would have taken offense at such a question.

The older man relaxed slightly, and Scott guessed that he had passed some kind of obscure test. "Makes no never mind to me," the oldster said. "Name's Zeke Cantrell."

Scott gripped the knobby hand and gave his own name.

Zeke eyed him up and down. "You looking for a particular kind of work?"

"I'm not looking for work right now."

Zeke seemed to physically chew over the answer. His lantern jaw worked strenuously. "Might be you'll find it anyway," he said obscurely. "Some kinds of work ain't available around here. Others are. Those kinds find you." He eyed Scott from top to bottom once again.

Scott opened his mouth to question the remark. The harsh sounds of men's voices cut him off. A woman's voice was raised in anger. Scott looked around.

Two customers had emerged from the general store and mounted to the wagon's seat. Scott had the impression of a stocky, balding man past middle age with a blond woman or girl at his side.

The three rowdies he had noticed earlier were no longer on the store's porch. They had moved into the street to bracket the wagon. One of them stood in front of the two old draft horses hitched to the wagon. He gripped their reins. His companions stood one on either side of the wagon.

Scott heard the girl's voice again lifted in anger. He glimpsed the leering grin of the burly fellow staring hungrily at her. Scott was moving forward before he quite realized it.

The man on the other side of the wagon was even larger than his companion. "You ain't welcome here, padre," he told the wagon's driver. He reached up as he spoke, and yanked one of the bundles of supplies from the wagon. It tumbled to the street. "Maybe you need some help packing." Sarcasm was harsh in his voice.

The driver stiffened. He was unarmed, and he said something in low tones to his persecutor. The big man hesitated, then lifted a threatening fist.

Scott could see the trio of rowdies better now. They all wore guns, but it was obvious that guns were not their specialty. These were rough-and-tumble boys. Their burly builds and battered faces proclaimed them as men more accustomed to fighting with their fists and booted feet than with their guns.

"You need any more help, padre?" the spokesman snarled.

"You may be the one who needs help, pal," Scott said.

He had halted several feet in back and slightly to one side of the bruiser holding the horses. The fellow twisted his head to see Scott. His hands were full with the big restless animals, and he could not release them to confront Scott.

The spokesman was the biggest of the trio. He glared at Scott from tiny eyes beneath a thick, sloping brow. He was bearded and mountainous, taller than Scott and much heavier. "Stay out of this!" he rumbled.

Scott shrugged. "Too late for that now." He was aware of the distressed, pretty face of the girl and the grim anger of the older man.

The third bruiser reached up for the girl with a big groping paw. She gasped in startled outrage. The older man made a sound of rage and tried to reach her tormentor. It was a mistake, because it distracted his attention from the bearded giant on his own side of the wagon.

The big man's hands shot up to grip clothing and flesh. With a heaving effort he hauled the older man completely out of the wagon and slammed him to the ground. The girl screamed.

Scott rushed forward and gripped the elbow of the man holding the horses. It kept him from turning as Scott whipped a fist into his kidneys. The hardcase's spine arched in agony. Grabbing him by the ears from behind, Scott yanked him backward across an out-stretched leg. The man hit the ground hard on his back. Scott had no time for niceties. The heel of his boot snapped the fellow's head sideways. He collapsed.

Both of the other men had started toward Scott. The girl was standing erect in the wagon. The older man was moving weakly on the ground.

The bearded giant rounded the wagon. He was on Scott's left. His face was barbarous in its savagery. "I won't be so easy, pilgrim," he spat.

"Neither will I," Scott said. He turned and went for the other man to his right.

Scott knew the first and most basic rule for fighting more than one opponent—stay away from the most dangerous foe and put the others out of the fight first. He had already dispatched one of his lesser opponents. He could not afford to lose his advantage.

The man on his right was obviously a tough, sea-soned brawler. His blocky fists were raised as he came in. His face was set and serious. Scott swung his foot in a sideward swipe. The edge of his boot caught the brawler's ankle from the outside. His leg faltered. Unexpected pain snarled from his features. His clenched fists dropped from in front of his face.

Scott went in over those lowered fists with a straight-arm left and a hooking right. Already off balance, the brawler staggered. Scott was conscious of the looming presence of the bearded giant close at his back. He clamped both hands on the staggering brawler's fore-arm, and with his feet set firmly, he swung the man around in a half circle. Free arm flailing, the brawler collided with his larger, oncoming companion.

Scott sank a left into the brawler's larded gut and then hooked again with his right to the jaw. The man's knees buckled. Then his falling body was shoved effort-lessly aside by a sweeping arm of the bearded giant. The huge man slammed his other fist around at Scott's face.

Scott saw the blow coming, but he was in too close. He dropped his chin to his chest and tried to duck in-side the blow. His timing was off, and he ducked full into the path of the massive fist. His head seemed to tear from his shoulders in a black concussion of pain. His Stetson went flying. He was spun out and away from his opponent. He dropped to one knee.

One hand was flat on the ground, and through it he felt the impact of the giant's rushing feet. The man's bulk loomed hugely over him. He tried to twist away. The big man's lifting knee caught him in the chest like a driven railroad tie. The impact rammed the air from him. It lifted him erect to meet the giant's locked fists hammering down to the back of his neck.

He was smashed flat on his face. A roaring was in his ears, and he knew he had to roll clear or die. The toe of the big man's boot drove agonizingly into his side. It half lifted him from the street, but it threw him clear momentarily.

Dimly Scott focused on the booted feet shuffling in for another kick. He heaved his whole body sideways against the big man's legs. His weight staggered his opponent. He got his feet under him and came surging up from the ground with an uppercutting fist. It met the giant's body at the V of his ribs and raised him onto his toes. Scott straightened and uppercut again, both fists together to the bearded jaw.

The big man growled like the bear he resembled, and he reached for Scott with mauling hands. Scott ducked beneath his grasp and, lifting one foot, he drove the flat of it to the back of the bearded giant's knee. That leg bent sharply.

Before his foe could turn, Scott ripped left and right to his kidneys. He felt the hard slabs of muscle beneath his fists. The big man grunted in pain. Scott swung his arms wide, tried to smash his fists together with the big man's skull in-between. His knuckles pounded against the giant's ears.

As the big man shook his head, Scott caught him at the hinge of the jaw with a driving right. The massive bulk faltered, and his arm swept around like a tree trunk. Scott crouched and felt the rush of air as it passed over him. He snapped a one-two combination into the man's body, then flung himself clear.

The giant's breath came in muffled grunts. Scott met the gaze of the sunken eyes. They had both absorbed damage. Scott was surprised that the man was still on his feet. He was surprised that he himself was still on his feet.

The big man lurched toward him. Scott didn't want to, but he went to meet him. He had to finish this before the other two were able to rejoin the fight. He was almost finished himself.

He feinted high with a right. His burly foe lifted his fists to cover. Scott kicked him solidly in the stomach. The big man cursed and lashed out, but without the awesome strength of his earlier blows.

Scott went after him with both fists working. It was like using a hammer to gradually demolish a boulder. Scott avoided the big man's weakened blows. He twisted blows of his own into the thick, vulnerable body. He drove his fists against jaw and temple. The big man swayed. Scott delivered a pistoning straight-arm right squarely between the sunken eyes. He hit so hard that he reeled back from the impact.

He barely managed to step aside as the big man toppled forward onto his face.

Scott turned on shaky legs. The other two rowdies were climbing to their feet. They looked uneasily from Scott to the older man who had been their intended victim. The latter had recovered from where the big man had thrown him in the street. Dusty, angry, he stood solidly in the wagon and menaced the pair grimly with a Winchester.

"Go away!" His voice carried, although it did not seem loud. "Leave us alone. There's been enough violence." Sadness as well as strength was evident in his tone.

With parting glances at their fallen partner, the pair moved unsteadily away. Scott became aware that a number of spectators had gathered. Some were townspeople. Others looked like early patrons of the saloons and gaming houses. Scott saw a striking, dark-haired woman at the door of the largest saloon. As his glance fell on her, she turned and disappeared inside. He was left with little more than an impression of her alluring beauty.

As the spectators dispersed, Scott wondered about their lack of attention. Normally, even a stranger such as he would have been congratulated heartily by Western townspeople for his victory against heavy odds. But these citizens had turned sullenly away. Was the rowdy trio so popular in this town? he wondered.

The older man laid the rifle aside, then hopped down from the wagon with a surprising agility. The pretty blond girl had already alighted from her seat. They hurried toward Scott.

"Are you all right?" The girl reached him first, with concern evident in her face.

"I'm fine," Scott told her. Unexpectedly, his legs faltered beneath him. They both caught him as he swayed. He was aware of the capable strength in the man's grip and of the determination in the girl's.

They helped him to the wagon, where he leaned gratefully against it. His strength was rapidly returning, but his whole body ached from the blows the big man had landed. Scott thought that it would not take many such impacts to kill a man.

"Ruth, see if the storekeep has something for him to drink," the man directed.

Scott started to protest, but the girl was already hurrying toward the store. He straightened from the wagon and got a good look at the other man for the first time.

He was stocky, with firm, well-defined features that spoke of the same strength Scott had felt in his hands and heard in his voice. Only a fringe of graying blond hair was left to him. He wore work clothes that were old but clean.

"Are *you* all right?" Scott asked.

The older man grinned with disarming warmth. "I've taken harder falls in my time," he said. He extended his hand. "I'm Reverend Samuel Prentiss. Most folks just call me Brother Sam."

Scott recalled the industrious youth hammering away at the church. Matt had told Scott that his father and sister were in town buying supplies. Scott should not have been surprised, but he was. "Scott Colton. I met your boy back down the trail a ways."

"Matthew?" A trace of disquiet had appeared in the firm brown eyes.

Scott nodded. "Yeah. I think he'll probably have that church finished by the time you get back out there."

Brother Sam grinned in relief. "He may at that," he agreed. "He's a hard worker." He grew more serious. "Ruth and I owe you some thanks."

Scott shrugged uneasily. Twice in one day now he had stepped in to help victims at the risk of his own life. It was not behavior with which he was entirely comfortable, considering his past. "Three hardcases against a man their senior and a girl just didn't set right with me," he said.

Brother Sam looked past him. The big bearded brawler was beginning to stir. "Poor lost souls," he murmured.

Scott saw genuine compassion in the brown eyes. He

recalled the same man standing erect in the wagon with his leveled Winchester. The Reverend Sam Prentiss was a man of definite contrasts.

"Here, I got you some lemonade." The girl, Ruth, had reappeared with a mug. "Drink some, then let me tend to your face. I've got a damp cloth."

Accepting the mug, Scott felt the brush of her fingertips against his hand. The cool, tart liquid tasted good in his parched mouth. While drinking, he stole a better look at the girl.

Her father's strength was there in her warm features, but it was a strength tempered with gentle femininity. She gazed at Scott with evident concern. Her soft, brown eyes were a shade lighter than her father's. The excitement of the past moments had brought an appealing flush to her cheeks. Her golden hair was pulled back, but a few strands had worked themselves fetchingly free. The sunlight sparkled on them. A modest and practical dress clothed her slender figure.

"Are you finished?" Her tone was puzzled.

Scott realized that he had half lowered the mug and stood holding it while he gazed at her like some moonstruck fool. "Sure, here," he said. "Thanks."

Hurriedly she took the cup and shoved it toward her father. He took it without comment. A slight grin lurked on his mouth.

"Let me see to your face," she said.

"No, it's all right," Scott protested.

"Nonsense, my boy," Brother Sam spoke up. "She's right. Let her take a look. That bruiser might have hurt you. It's hard to tell under all that dirt."

Scott became aware that his face was aching painfully. One side of it felt swollen, and he lifted a hand to it.

"Quit that." Ruth caught his wrist and drew his hand down. "Sit here on the wagon wheel."

Scott complied. He glimpsed the pastor's widening grin. Obviously his daughter's commanding ways were not new to Brother Sam.

She moved close to him. Her warm brown eyes narrowed in concentration as she studied his face. Scott was intensely aware of her nearness. He sensed her softness and smelled her lilac scent.

She lifted a hand to his face. Her touch was as light as a breeze. Gently she applied the damp cloth. Scott winced.

"I'm sorry," she said, "but you'll have to hold still."

Scott relaxed and submitted to her ministrations. The touch of the cloth was soothing to his sore face. Her compelling feminine presence seemed to engulf him. He felt her fingers probe the back of his neck.

Too soon to please Scott, she drew back and said, "There, that should do it." She was slightly breathless and her flush had deepened. "I'm sure you'll recover quickly," she said.

Now that her task was done, she appeared to regain some of her gentle modesty. She dropped her gaze from Scott's, and she collected the mug from her father and placed it and the cloth on the porch of the store.

"Ruth, I'd like you to meet Scott Colton, our benefactor," Brother Sam announced as she turned back to them.

"How can we ever thank you?" she said.

"Somebody else would have stepped in if I hadn't," Scott told her. "I just happened to be closest."

"No, I don't think anyone else would have helped us." She seemed about to say more, but she glanced at her father and fell silent.

Scott turned to the reverend. "Your boy said you had enemies in these parts, pastor," he probed.

Brother Sam nodded. "So it would seem. Apparently not everyone is in favor of having a church here in Meridian." He didn't seem disposed to dwell on the subject. "You're new in town, aren't you?" he asked.

"Just rode in."

As Brother Sam studied him, Scott guessed that the pastor was just becoming aware that their rescuer bore the same hard stamp as their attackers.

"We owe you a debt, Mr. Colton. We'd be honored if you'd have dinner with us this evening."

Scott noticed that Ruth's flush had deepened again. "All right," he accepted awkwardly. "I guess so." Instantly he regretted his acceptance. What did he know about having dinner with a preacher man and his family?

"Good, good." Brother Sam's satisfaction seemed genuine. "You know where the church is. Ride out a little after dusk. That should give us plenty of time." The teasing smile came back to him. "Ruth's as good a cook as she is a nurse."

"Father!" Ruth cried softly. She would not look at Scott. Instead, she went back to the porch to return the mug and the cloth to the storekeeper.

Suddenly Scott guessed that she was not more than two or three years older than her brother. She had the poise of an older woman except for her girlish lapse at her father's inexplicable teasing. Scott figured that her poise must have come from being forced to serve as the woman in a family of two men after her mother's death. He didn't doubt that she had done a good job.

"We'll see you later, then." Brother Sam grasped his hand in parting. Ruth reappeared and hurried to mount to the wagon seat after replacing the fallen bundle.

The reverend climbed up more slowly. His fall might have been paining him more than he had let on, Scott thought, but he took the reins with a capable firmness. Scott stepped to the porch of the store as the wagon went by. Brother Sam gave him a friendly wave, and Scott imagined that he glimpsed Ruth's pretty face turn briefly back toward him.

He watched the wagon go. Feeling an odd perplexity, he shook his head to dispel it. His former opponents had disappeared, and he headed back toward the stable.

Zeke was there to grin amiably at him. "Pretty good," he complimented. "Those boys are tough."

"Yeah." Scott rubbed at his sore ribs. "Who were they, anyway?"

"Land Talbot's boys. Do you know Talbot?"

"Met him in passing, you might say. What's his game?"

Zeke shrugged his bony shoulders. "Pretty near anything he wants it to be."

"Owlhoot?"

Zeke shrugged again. "You didn't hear me say it. Him and his pack hole up a ways out of town. They come and go here pretty much as they please. Every so often a stagecoach or some bank elsewhere in the

Territory gets held up by masked men. Talbot and his crew generally show up here not long afterward with plenty to spend. Nobody ever connects them with the robberies, though."

"Has anybody ever tried?"

Zeke's jaws worked wordlessly for a moment before he replied. "Heck Thomas, the U.S. marshal up at Guthrie, sent a man out here a few months back. He up and disappeared and nobody's seen him since."

"There's no other law here?"

"Only old Heck, and he's got his hands full up in Guthrie most times." Zeke looked at him speculatively. "You say you ran into Land Talbot and his boys?"

"Yeah, back up the trail a piece."

Zeke clearly wanted some further explanation. When none was forthcoming, he went on, "They're a rough bunch. Talbot himself ain't no greenhorn, and his right arm's a slick gunny name of Strike Foster. And guns ain't all that Foster's good with. He's got this danged throwing stick he calls a boomerang. Said he picked it up in Australia, wherever that is. He can do the darnedest things with that stick."

"I've seen him use it," Scott said. He remembered Hunting Wolf tumbling head over heels beneath the weapon's impact. "What does Talbot have against the reverend?"

"Maybe he just don't like churches."

From the corner of his eye, Scott saw a figure striding determinedly across the street toward them. His nerves were still on edge. He turned sharply, then relaxed a bit.

The man approaching wore the livery of a barkeep

in a fancy saloon. He halted near them. Scott felt tension ease back into him. Despite the man's garb, something in the hard cast of his face indicated that maybe he had not always followed such a genteel trade.

"Miss Belle wants to see you, friend," he said to Scott without preamble. He didn't appear particularly pleased with his role as messenger boy.

"Who?" Scott asked bluntly.

"Miss Belle Tanner," the barkeep answered with irritation. "She owns the Dark Lady." He jerked his head toward the ornate facade of one of the larger saloons across the street.

It was the same saloon where Scott had glimpsed the alluring woman after the fight. Had that been the mysterious Belle Tanner? "Why does she want to see me?"

The barkeep shrugged. "She don't tell me her secrets."

Scott looked at the saloon, then shot a questioning glance at Zeke. The stable owner grinned a crooked grin with little humor in it. "May as well go along with the man," he advised. "Ain't nobody says no to Miss Belle in this town."

Scott followed the sullen barkeep toward the saloon.

Chapter Two

The interior of the Dark Lady matched the elaborate facade out front. A hand-carved hardwood
bar stretched the length of one wall. Manning it during
the busy hours would take at least four bartenders,
Scott estimated.

At the moment business was slow. A few cowhands
and drifters, attended by a lackadaisical pair of bar
girls, were seated at the closely packed tables. There
was a stage for entertainment and a few gaming tables,
none of them occupied currently. Gaudy paintings
adorned the walls. A long mirror mounted behind the
bar gave the large room an impression of even greater
size. At the back of the room a wide circular staircase
swept up to a balcony lined with closed doors.

The barkeep led Scott toward the stairway, but they
did not ascend it. As they drew near, Scott noticed a
massive ornate wooden door in the shadows behind it.
The barkeep knocked respectfully, and a woman's voice
answered from inside. The barkeep opened the door

and pushed it wide. He moved out of the way so that Scott could pass.

Scott stepped into an elegant combination sitting room and office. Perfume and some other faint, harsh scent touched his nostrils. A massive mahogany desk was facing the door to one side. The striking dark-haired woman rose smoothly from where she sat behind it. "That will be all, Johnny," she said.

The barkeep had been hovering in the open doorway. He withdrew, his face expressionless. The door clicked shut.

Scott shifted his gaze back to his hostess. She had moved from behind the desk to stand in front of a bar with a comprehensive selection of bottles. She seemed to pose there as if inviting inspection of her and her surroundings.

On the wall behind the bar was a full-length painting of a woman reclining on a plush chaise longue. The picture was breathtakingly seductive. Filmy veils concealed certain areas of the woman's full figure. It took Scott a long moment to realize that the woman in the painting was the same woman who stood before him in the flesh.

Her graceful posture in front of the painting was a deliberate one, he realized. It emphasized that, as stunning as the revealing portrait of her might be, this woman, fully dressed in real life, was far more compelling.

She wore a simple black dress with a swathe of what must be diamonds at her throat. Her dark hair was done up in an elaborate coiffure above a face of regal beauty. Skillfully applied cosmetics served only to emphasize the beauty. She was no longer a young girl, but the matter of her age was submerged and lost in the sheer beguiling impact of her presence.

"Hello," she said with a slight tilting of her head. Her voice was throaty. It was a singer's voice. "I'm Belle Tanner. Welcome to the Dark Lady."

Scott felt an awareness that he was being manipulated like an inexperienced schoolboy by this captivating woman and her subtle, alluring poses.

"Ma'am," he murmured with deliberate politeness, and doffed his hat.

Amusement sparkled in her dark eyes. "No need to be so formal." She offered him no alternative form of address, however. Instead she turned gracefully to the bar. "Let me get you a drink." She picked up one of the bottles.

"No, thanks," Scott said.

"Suit yourself." She appeared undisturbed at his refusal. "I thought you might be thirsty." She manipulated bottle and glass with familiar efficiency. Drink in hand, she turned back to face him. "I know I am." She took a casual sip, then studied him over the rim of her glass.

Scott pulled his eyes away from her. The room was designed for entertainment as well as business. Which did she have in mind for him?

Belle Tanner crossed to a plush chaise longue that might have been the one in the painting. She settled onto it, shoulder pressed against its back, her feet on the floor.

"Please sit down." She gestured smoothly with the

glass. "There." She indicated an upholstered chair near the foot of the longue.

As Scott stepped toward it, a guttural growl locked him in his tracks. The gray beast rose up from behind the longue in a single easy movement. Trembling lips peeled back from gleaming fangs. The animal was more wolf than dog, and all the more dangerous because of it. He understood now the faint bestial scent that lurked in the room.

Standing, the wolf dog's shoulder was taller than the chaise longue. It snarled and came around it in two stiff-legged steps.

"Lobo!" The woman's voice echoed sharply in the room.

The beast froze. Scott could see the muscles vibrating beneath the grayish coat. The malevolent yellow eyes glared at him. He lifted his hand casually toward the butt of the .45.

"Don't!" Belle snapped. "He'd be on you before you cleared leather. I've seen him do it." She said to the dog, "Lobo! Back! Down!"

Some of the vibrant savagery seemed to flow out of the animal. Obediently he retreated to his former spot behind the chaise. Scott lifted his gaze to the woman. His throat was dry.

"Lobo's my bodyguard," she explained. "He misunderstood when you moved toward me."

She did not apologize, and Scott's movement had been at her invitation. He wondered if he had been set up for the confrontation. Had she manipulated him as deftly as the big dog?

"I got him when he was a pup," she continued. "He's

part wolf. A friend of mine who worked at a carnival gave him to me. He trained him for me too. Lobo obeys only my commands." Arrogance underscored her words.

Scott looked again at the wolf dog. He felt a sadness for the living weapon that Belle Tanner and her nameless friend had made of the animal. "I'm sure you sleep comfortably," he said.

"That's right. Sit down. He won't bother you now."

Scott settled into the embrace of the chair. It was so deep that he knew he would have trouble rising from it or drawing his gun in an emergency. He could not shake his prickling awareness of the wolf dog's ominous presence.

"I don't know your name," she said.

"Scott Colton."

She repeated it thoughtfully. "I like it." Her dark eyes appraised him. "I saw you fight."

Scott recalled glimpsing her outside the saloon. What had been her interest in the fight? Or did she simply like to watch street brawls? He would not have been surprised if such was the case. He shrugged in response to her comment.

"You're good with your fists." She sipped at her drink. Her eyes never left him.

"I took them by surprise," Scott said. "They weren't expecting a fight."

"You look like you're fast with a gun too."

Scott glanced where Lobo watched him expectantly through half-lidded eyes. "Maybe even faster than your dog," he said.

"No," she said firmly. "No one's that fast."

Scott regretted his remark. He was trying to leave his past behind. He had no business bragging about his skills with a gun. Where was this conversation going? he wondered with growing irritation.

She seemed to read his thought. "I asked you over here because I think I might have a place for you on my payroll."

"As what?" he asked. "A bartender?"

"No." She shook her head in dismissal of the idea. "Let me explain." She settled back in the chaise, the diamonds gleaming on her ivory neck. "When I came to this town five years ago, I didn't have anything to my name but the clothes I wore." Her voice seemed to have grown rougher, less cultured. "I started out working at this saloon. I sang and hustled drinks." Her dark eyes grew moody, as if she considered adding something more. But she decided against it. "Now I own the saloon." She announced it as if challenging him. "I also own a controlling interest in the bank, two of the hotels here in town, and the freight office. I'm the largest property owner in town."

"A woman of means," Scott commented.

"That's right, and it's not easy holding that much property in a town like this, particularly for a woman. Do you understand what I mean?"

She was right, Scott mused. It would take an extraordinary and strong-willed woman to acquire and hold such assets in a wide-open town like Meridian. But Belle Tanner was obviously such a woman. "You seem to be doing all right," he told her.

"Oh, I am," she was quick to assure him. "Don't misunderstand me, I can take care of myself and my property."

Scott didn't doubt it. He guessed that she would also be a formidable opponent across a poker table. And few men would have the nerve to try anything against her personally when faced with the menacing presence of Lobo.

"But I need good men to look after my interests," she went on. "I think you're the kind of man I need."

"A fighting man?" Scott inquired sourly. "Someone good with his fists and his gun?"

"That helps," she responded immediately. "But it's just a part of it. I can buy that kind of talent. In fact, I've got a number of 'fighting men,' as you call them, on my payroll right now. But I also need someone who can make decisions and who will think before he resorts to force. I can read men pretty well. I've had a lot of experience. And I'm usually accurate in what I read."

He sensed a withdrawal of the manipulative powers she had been trying to wield against him. Maybe her posing and the trick with the dog had been no more than her way of sizing up a man. Certainly a woman in her position would have developed an ability to handle men and to test their mettle in ways other than their abilities in a fight. Apparently he had passed her tests.

"You might be reading more in me than what's really there," he warned.

Her smile carried confidence and a bit of affection. "I don't think so."

His dubious talents were certainly in high demand hereabouts, Scott reflected. He recalled Zeke Cantrell's obscure remarks about work finding him whether he wanted it or not. First there had been Land Talbot, and now this alluring woman with offers of employment. But Belle Tanner's proposal was far different from Talbot's suggestion that he join the ranks of his outlaw gang.

"I'm not even looking for work," he told her.

That smile flashed back, confident and natural. "Well, think about it," she urged.

Scott *was* thinking about it, and despite himself, he found her proposal attractive. The idea of working for her carried its own appeal. The pay, he had no doubt, would be good, probably far better than he had ever made before. And the job would also be a cut above the kind of work he had done in the past, even though it still smacked of hiring out his gun. But what other talents did he have?

"I'm interested," she said. "What made you get involved when those men were bothering the preacher?" She appeared curiously intent on his answer.

Scott looked away uncomfortably. Then he shifted his gaze back. "It seemed like the thing to do, I guess. Nobody else was willing to take a hand."

"The reverend and his family aren't particularly welcome here."

"Why is that?"

"This town isn't ready for a church. Personally, I don't care one way or the other if he starts one. But I can tell you, he's wasting his time."

"He doesn't think so."

"Well, he'll figure it out eventually, and then he'll move on." She seemed ready to dismiss the subject.

Remembering the strength and determination he had

seen in the pastor and his children, Scott didn't agree with her opinion, but he kept the thought to himself.

"Come by the bar this evening and have a drink on the house," she said. "Maybe you'll be thirsty by then and will have made up your mind." Her smile was gently teasing.

Scott recalled his acceptance of Brother Sam's dinner invitation. "I'll see," he replied.

The entire Prentiss family, he reflected, had been put off by his appearance as a man who lived by the gun. Still, they had extended their hospitality to him. What would they think of him if he accepted Belle Tanner's offer? Working for her, he would still be no more than a highly paid hired gun. The misgivings of the Prentiss family would be confirmed. The thought was unpleasant.

Belle Tanner was watching him closely. Scott had the sudden disturbing impression that she could discern his thoughts. The opinions of a preacher man and his two children shouldn't mean anything to him, he thought almost angrily. He remembered the brown eyes of Ruth Prentiss and her innocent embarrassment at her father's teasing.

"I guess I'll hold off a spell on working for you, ma'am," he told her. "Like I said, I'm not looking for work right now."

Something stirred in the depths of her dark eyes. On the floor, Lobo lifted his head. "I'm disappointed." She pouted slightly.

"Thanks, anyway." It was time for him to go, Scott decided. As he rose from the embrace of the plush chair, Lobo's head lifted higher and his ears pricked alert. Despite his earlier boast, Scott had no desire to try the dog's speed against his own.

"Stay, Lobo," she murmured without looking at the beast. "Keep my offer in mind," she told Scott. "It'll still be open if you change your mind."

"Yes, ma'am."

"And call me Belle." She gave him that little teasing smile again.

He nodded, and was suddenly eager to be gone. She made no move to rise from the chaise as he let himself out. He could feel her eyes and those of the wolf dog on his back even after the door closed behind him. Crossing the saloon, he was aware of Johnny watching him from behind the bar.

Outside, Scott crossed to the stable, where he found Zeke Cantrell in the dim interior. The old hostler was brushing the trail grime from his sorrel mare. She stood relaxed, enjoying the attention.

Zeke glanced around as he came in. He eyed Scott up and down. "She left you in one piece," he commented.

"Her dog almost didn't," Scott returned.

Zeke spat. "Poor danged wolf oughta be running the prairie, not shut up in her fancy bedchamber, waiting to eat alive any man she sics him onto." He cocked his head at Scott. "I seen that animal kill a man once."

"I don't doubt it."

Zeke turned away from the mare and leaned his shoulders comfortably against her flank. She did not stir. "It was right out there on the street in plain daylight. This rowdy had taken a yearning for Miss Belle in the bar the night before. She cut him off cold like she does all the lowlifes that take after her. She finally had him thrown out. Well, he was still liquored up the next morning and made a grab for her when she went by on the street." Zeke spat again. "That dog had him down before he could do much more than scream. She didn't call him off until it was too late."

"That rooming house you recommended," he cut in on Zeke's reminiscing. "What was it called?"

"Didn't say," Zeke answered. "But it's the Hollis House over yonder."

"Who owns it?"

"Fellow named Mort Hollis." Zeke studied Scott shrewdly.

"Thanks," Scott told him. "I'll be needing the mare a little bit later."

"She'll be here, fat and sassy," Zeke promised.

After a bath and a shave at the Hollis House, Scott took a leisurely stroll around the town. Activity picked up as the afternoon drew to a close. Cowhands, local workers, and businessmen from Guthrie began to patronize the various entertainment establishments lining the main street. Pale, dandyish gamblers and painted, underdressed bar girls emerged from their lairs to prey on them. Tense-eyed gunhawks roamed, or lounged, or indulged in the vices offered. Scott wondered how many of them were on Belle's payroll. There seemed to be lots of them for a town the size of Meridian.

Curious and gauging glances were cast at him. He realized that the tale of his fight with the ruffians and his audience with Belle Tanner must have made the rounds. He kept a wary eye for his opponents from that afternoon, but saw no sign of them.

He noticed with some interest the large number of Negroes among the town's populace. There was a movement afoot to have the Territory declared a separate Negro state, and he wondered if the U.S. Congress would approve such a measure. It seemed doubtful.

Zeke had the sorrel mare saddled when Scott returned to the stable. The girth was still loose. Zeke cinched it tight and handed Scott the reins.

Scott could smell food cooking before he reached the church. His stomach rumbled to remind him that he hadn't bothered with eating since a dry breakfast on the trail that morning.

A tent had been pitched beside the frame of the church. Scott glimpsed Ruth's hurried disappearance inside it as he reined up the sorrel. Matt came forward from the campfire as he dismounted.

"I'll take your horse," the youth offered with restrained eagerness. His blond hair was combed, and he wore clean faded denims and a starched white shirt.

"Thanks." Scott surrendered the reins.

"I'm glad you came," Matt rushed on. "Pa and Ruth told me what happened in town. I wish I could've helped."

"I expect your pa thinks you were helping plenty by working on the church while he was gone."

Matt nodded with somewhat less enthusiasm. "Ruth's not quite ready. She's been busy fixing dinner. There's Pa now."

The elder Prentiss had appeared from within the

framework of the church. He came briskly forward. His smile was warm. He, too, wore clean clothes, but not the dark suit Scott had somehow expected. "Welcome, welcome." He clasped Scott's hand in both of his.

Scott felt suddenly awkward and out of place. He regretted having come. He had nothing in common with this dedicated man of God and his sheltered son. But it was too late to back out.

He allowed himself to be ushered to the fire. He noted a Winchester leaning against the wagon. Another rifle was near the fire. It occurred to him that, even with the Winchesters, Prentiss and his offspring were ill-equipped to deal with a hostile visit by Land Talbot and his pack. He glanced about at the surrounding woods in the gathering dusk.

They were barely seated when Ruth emerged from the tent. Scott caught his breath. She wore a simple blue dress that modestly displayed her slender form. Her blond hair was done up. It glinted golden in the firelight.

She set about serving them with a bustling efficiency. Scott tried to catch her eye and failed. She seemed intent on handling the meal preparations. Scott received a plate with a thick slice of fried ham, fried potatoes, a generous helping of beans, and two enormous biscuits. His mouth watered. He caught himself in time as Brother Sam solemnly bowed his head and uttered a blessing.

Only when all three males were eating did Ruth serve herself. Then she settled gracefully to the ground, tucking her legs under her dress. She was seated by her brother, across the fire from Scott. Despite his hunger,

Scott found his eyes drawn to her lovely features across the flickering flames. More than once during the meal, she jumped to her feet to pour coffee or offer second helpings. Scott watched her smooth, unaffected movements.

"Excellent dinner, Ruth," Brother Sam said at last as he wiped his mouth with his napkin. He leaned back from his empty plate and patted his midriff in satisfaction.

Scott's belly was fuller than it had been in weeks. He added his own compliments. For the first time Ruth met his gaze. She gave him a shy smile before bending quickly to collect Matt's plate. Scott thought it might be the fire that brought the flush to her features. He was glad he had come.

"Will you be staying around here very long?" Matt asked.

"I don't know yet," Scott answered. "Maybe."

"Are you looking for work?" Brother Sam said.

Scott wondered if there were devious levels to the question, but Brother Sam's face was open and frank. "No," Scott told him. On impulse he added, "I did get an offer, though."

"Is that right? Who from?"

"Belle Tanner." Scott saw Ruth stiffen for just a moment as she went about her cleanup work.

"Did you accept it?" Brother Sam asked.

"No," Scott answered. He was glad he could make the reply. "I turned her down."

Ruth straightened with the last of the dishes in her hands. "I'll be right back," she said breathlessly. She hurried away toward the tent.

"Belle Tanner seems to be quite a power in Meridian," Brother Sam commented. "What she doesn't own, she influences."

"So I gathered," Scott agreed.

"I've never met the woman."

"I doubt that you'll see her in church."

"You're probably right," Brother Sam admitted. "However, I'll go out of my way to invite her. A church should be open to everyone."

"Did you pastor a church before coming here?" Scott asked. He was curious about Brother Sam's past.

"Several at one time or another," Sam told him. His voice grew reflective. "I was probably a couple of years younger than you when I first got the call to preach. I rode the circuit in Arizona until I met Alice. After we got married, I decided I needed to settle down, especially when Ruth came along. From then on, I stuck to one church at a time."

Scott glanced at Matt. The youth was watching his father intently. Scott sensed that they were reliving shared memories for a brief, wishful moment.

"We were in Tucson when Alice went home to the Lord," Brother Sam continued. "She was a good wife and a good mother, but her health had gotten bad over the last few years. She took pneumonia and they couldn't save her."

"I'm sorry," Scott said awkwardly.

Brother Sam nodded his acceptance of the sentiment. "Things weren't the same after that. I couldn't stay in Tucson. I needed a new beginning, I suppose. I'd heard about the land run that opened these parts. Millions of acres settled in one day." He shook his head in wonder.

"I resigned from the church I was pastoring there, and the kids and I came out here. In Guthrie we heard that Meridian didn't have a church. When we got here, I knew this was where I was supposed to be." He stared into the flames as if seeing some personal vision. "I know there's a need for a church here. I know it in my heart and in my soul. And I'll see one built here, or die trying."

"But it's not fair!" Matt cried suddenly. "We're not hurting anybody! Why are they trying to stop us?"

Brother Sam regarded his son somberly. Scott understood that this was not a new issue between them. Perhaps it explained the undercurrent of unhappiness he had detected in Matt that afternoon.

"Persecution is nothing new for those following the right path," Brother Sam said.

"But what would've happened to you and Ruth this afternoon if Scott hadn't been there?" Matt demanded.

"We don't have to worry about that, do we?"

Matt lapsed into a sullen silence. Scott sensed that the boy's dedication to his father and his father's calling was at war with his resentment at the mistreatment and hostility they were encountering.

"Nothing worthwhile ever comes free," Scott said to him. "If it's worthwhile, you have to work for it, and sometimes you have to fight for it. You just need to be careful that you don't fight for the wrong things." He felt Brother Sam's eyes on him.

He looked up as Ruth came back from the direction of the tent. "I'm sorry," she apologized. "I wanted to get the dishes cleaned some before they sat for very long." She settled once more beside the fire with that natural grace. This time she was midway between Scott and her brother. "Has Father been telling you all about the church?"

Her coming had banished the hovering spirit of depression. Scott found himself returning her warm smile. "He told me some about your home," he answered.

"This is home now," she said brightly. "I think things will get much better once the church is completed."

Scott wondered if she had sensed the tension between father and son, and if her cheerfulness was a deliberate attempt to lessen the strain. Yet, he could tell that her optimism was genuine. It appeared to have overcome her earlier shyness.

"Where are you from, Scott?" she asked.

"Up Kansas way," he answered vaguely. He would have resented the question from a man, but coming from her, it was acceptable, and even pleasing. But his past was not something he wanted to discuss.

"What had you been doing up there before you came down here?" she probed further.

"Fighting for the wrong things," Scott said.

Matt looked at him sharply, but didn't speak.

Ruth's expression was puzzled. She didn't pursue the matter. "What brought you down here?"

Her face had a bewitching beauty in the fire-tossed shadows. "I guess I'm like your pa," Scott told her. "Looking for a new beginning."

He thought she relaxed slightly at his answer. "I hope you find it," she said softly.

"There's a future here." Brother Sam's tone bespoke his confidence. "When they fired the gun to start the land run back in '89, fifty thousand settlers raced to stake a claim in the unassigned lands. Guthrie and Meridian grew up overnight. Now Guthrie can lay claim to being one of the finest capitals in the whole country. That's the kind of spirit it takes to make a territory into a state. And statehood's not far off. There'll be a need for strong men and women and good churches and schools and businesses to build that state."

"Father, you're not in church," Ruth chided. "You don't need to preach."

Brother Sam grinned self-consciously. He glanced fondly at his daughter. "Sorry if I get started like that," he apologized to Scott. "But I do think there's a marvelous opportunity here for someone willing to work for it."

A chance for a new beginning, Scott mused. But how could he make his way? His scant savings would soon be gone. He had no skills or talents beyond the .45 on his hip. He thought of Belle Tanner and her intriguing offer. Then he dismissed the thought. There would be no new beginning with what she offered, only a continuation of the past he wanted to put behind him.

"The animosity here does puzzle me, however," Brother Sam admitted. Apparently he had not ignored Matt's earlier concerns. "I've never encountered this kind of opposition before."

Ruth nodded, her brow furrowed in thought. "It was almost like those men today were waiting for us." She shuddered.

The trio *had* been waiting for them, Scott reflected. He recalled his earlier thought that the opposition to

Brother Sam's plans seemed well organized. "What do you know about Land Talbot?" he asked.

"Not much," Brother Sam answered. "He apparently leads some kind of gang of owlhoots in this area. The townspeople are scared of him. I guess Matt told you about him and his men coming by here this morning."

Scott nodded. "I think those rowdies in town were part of his crew."

Ruth gasped. And her father frowned. "You're sure?" he probed.

Scott shrugged. "Pretty sure. Any idea why he'd want you run out of town?"

"None. Maybe he just doesn't care for churches."

"That's a fairly good bet," Scott agreed drily.

"You sound like you know him," Brother Sam suggested.

"I know his breed, and he's a bad one by even that standard." Scott recalled the deceptively handsome face of Land Talbot. He had read in that face the extremes of anger and cruelty of which its owner was capable. "I tangled a little bit with him and some of his boys back up the trail today."

Their faces gazed at him inquiringly.

"It was nothing important," he answered their unspoken queries. He did not want to say that he had shot a man that morning, even if he had only shot to wound.

"What do you make of Talbot?" Brother Sam inquired.

"He's mean. He'll try to take whatever he wants from whoever has it." It occurred to him again that this family was ill-prepared to deal with the likes of Land Talbot and his pack. He looked into the night beyond the skeletal frame of the church. Darkness had surrounded the camp while they talked.

It was getting late, and Scott said, "I appreciate the hospitality. I guess I better be going." He got to his feet.

"I'll get your horse," Ruth offered quickly. Scott caught a look of surprise on her brother's face. Ruth headed toward where the mare was tied.

Brother Sam rose stiffly to his feet. Obviously he was feeling the effects of the fall he had taken during the encounter with the brawlers. "Remember, Sunday is the day after tomorrow," he said. "I'll expect you here for our services."

Scott nodded. The prospect did not seem as disquieting as it had earlier. He shook hands with father and son. Ruth was waiting a little distance away with his mare, and he went over to her. She smiled with some of her earlier shyness as she offered him the reins. Briefly he felt her warm skin brush his as he accepted them. She did not release her hold immediately.

"I'm glad I came," Scott told her.

Her smile brightened. "So am I." Reluctantly, Scott thought, she relinquished the reins to him. He suddenly did not want to part from her. "I hope you'll come back to see—us," she told him softly.

Scott tried to find somewhere to look other than into her compelling eyes. He could see the branches of trees etched against the stars in the night sky. When he turned his gaze back to her, she was watching him silently. Her lips were parted slightly.

Scott groped for words. "You reckon your pa and

Matt could use some help building the church?" he managed finally.

Her smile flashed warm in the night. "I'm sure they could."

Scott nodded. His throat had gone dry suddenly. He eased the mare clear and mounted. He looked down at Ruth. She moved very close to the mare's side. "Maybe I'll be out to give them a hand," he said. His words sounded awkward in his ears.

"Okay," she whispered.

He did not want to leave the little area of light from the fire. But he turned the mare and rode into the darkness.

Chapter Three

How long had it been since he had worked up a sweat like this? Scott wondered. Carefully he tapped the head of the nail with the hammer to set it in the wood, and then he pounded it home with sure, hard strokes. His arm muscles ached from his countless repetitions of the act during the course of the day. But it was the satisfying ache of hard, honest work.

Feeling Matt's gaze on him, he glanced around to where the youth worked beside him. Once again Matt was stripped to the waist. Scott had shed his own shirt as the afternoon heat began to build.

Matt's grin carried the easy companionship of two men working to one purpose. Scott found himself returning it automatically.

"Here, now, you two look like you're having too much fun doing this," Brother Sam said as he rounded the corner of the church. He carried a hammer, and he stepped back and tilted his head to inspect the church. "It's coming," he said with satisfaction. "Scott, if you'd gotten here a week earlier, we might have had services inside tomorrow morning."

"I think a church service out-of-doors is fun," Ruth said from behind them. "I brought you some lemonade. The jug's been in the creek, so it should be cool."

Scott turned to look at her. She had come from the tent and was carrying three mugs and the jug. Her hair was pulled back from her face, as when he first saw her in town the day before. A few golden strands were teased by the light breeze. She wore a long, loose skirt and a simple blouse. Scott thought she looked wholesome and appealing. Little lights sparkled in her eyes.

He recalled suddenly that he was bare to the waist. He reached for his shirt and shrugged self-consciously into it before accepting a mug from her. She poured for each of them.

Brother Sam smacked his lips. "Bless you, daughter, for knowing what a thirsty man needs." His tone was teasing.

"Yeah, thanks, sis," Matt added between sips.

"The church looks wonderful," Ruth said, beaming at all of them. Scott imagined that her gaze lingered longest on him. "I just know we'll be proud of it."

"Scott's been a big help." Brother Sam drained the last of his lemonade. "Speaking of which, do either of you boys have any nails left? I've run out."

Scott retrieved the can of nails he and Matt had been sharing. "We're running low," he reported.

"That's what I was expecting. I'm afraid I miscalculated at the store yesterday and didn't purchase another keg of nails. I thought we had enough to last us into

next week. Of course, I wasn't expecting such worthy
assistance."

"I'll ride into town and pick up a keg," Scott volunteered. "That way we'll have plenty, come Monday
morning." It seemed natural to include himself as a part
of things.

"If you're going, you'd better hurry before the store
closes," Ruth advised.

"Right." Scott finished buttoning his shirt. He
stuffed the shirttails into his denims under his gun belt.
The .45 rode in its customary place at his side.
Throughout the long day's work, he had not removed
it, telling himself it was just a precaution in case of trouble. But he had worn it too long to feel at ease without
it.

He saddled the sorrel and swung up onto her. He
reined up as Ruth came near his stirrup. "Hurry back."
She smiled up at him. "I'm starting dinner."

Scott took along the image of her warm smile as he
rode out. He had come to their camp early that morning. Uneasiness had plagued him as he rode out from
town. Was he making a fool of himself by returning like
this to help them build a church? Had the soft stirrings
he'd sensed between himself and Ruth been no more
than his imagination? But the Prentiss family had
greeted him warmly, and the day spent working on the
church had been the most satisfying he could recall in
a long time. He was sorry that the day was drawing to
a close.

The Saturday-night crowd of cowboys, farmers, businessmen, and scavengers was already gathering in Meridian. A trio of mounted cowhands raced past Scott

at the edge of town. He followed their shouts and laughter on into town. The trio disappeared into the Dark Lady as he rode past. Belle Tanner would do a good business tonight, he surmised. He realized that he had not thought all day of the woman or her offer.

At the general store, Scott placed his order and charged it to the Prentiss account. The balding storekeeper vanished into the back of the store. In a moment he reappeared. He grunted as he hefted the small keg of nails up onto the counter.

"Will that do it?" he asked without smiling.

"Yep."

"I hear you're working with the preacher."

"Just helping out some," Scott told him.

The storekeep nodded a little grimly. "Well, you might tell the preacher that his credit is getting stretched kind of thin." His eyes shifted away from Scott's. "Just tell him I may not be able to carry him much longer."

"That didn't seem to bother you yesterday when you sold him a wagon full of supplies."

"Well, I, uh, had a chance to do the books since then." The fellow moved uncomfortably.

"Is Reverend Prentiss far behind on his bill?" Scott asked. Being in debt didn't sound like Brother Sam.

"Well, no," the storekeeper admitted. He appeared sorry he had ever begun the conversation. He was practically stammering as he continued, "But I've got to watch things like that."

Scott frowned at him until he ducked his head. "Funny way to run a business." Scott hefted the keg under his arm and went out of the store.

He lashed the keg behind his saddle. Hoofbeats pounded in the street, and he saw a dozen riders coming at a gallop. He felt his muscles harden. The commanding figure at the head of the riders was familiar. It was Land Talbot.

Talbot's roving glance fell on Scott. As he hauled his big Appaloosa hard over, the riders in his wake followed suit. Scott saw Strike Foster urge his horse up almost even with Talbot's animal. The unruly pack came to a dust-stirring halt in front of Scott. They seemed to fill the street.

Talbot's followers were of the same ilk as the men whom Scott had encountered with him on the range. Scott recognized several of those men from their first meeting. The wounded man was not with them. The tension coiled in Scott. This was a hard crew and he was desperately outnumbered.

He looked up at Talbot's handsome face. He was aware of the pale, menacing presence of Strike Foster at Talbot's side.

Talbot tilted back the brim of his brown Stetson. He was again clad in a businessman's suit. "I heard you were in town, Colton," he said.

"It's not a secret." Scott wondered if this was Talbot's whole pack. He didn't see the three bruisers among the riders.

"You sure you like it around here?" Talbot asked conversationally.

"Suits me fine," Scott told him. "Except for the trash in the streets."

Talbot stiffened. Suddenly his face was no longer

handsome. "You may not like it much longer," he said flatly.

"We'll see." It was stupid to bait this man with his pack of gunsels behind him, Scott knew, but something in him would not let him back down.

"You want me to show him how much he won't like it, boss?" Strike Foster asked. He held the curved throwing club—the boomerang—across his saddle horn in his white hands.

"He'll learn soon enough," Talbot told the gunfighter. Then he said to Scott, "I understand you're working for the preacher now."

Everybody seemed to know his business, Scott mused. "I'm giving him a hand," he admitted.

Talbot's lip lifted in a sneer. "That's peculiar work for a gunman."

"I told you, I'm out of that line of work," Scott said evenly. "What's your grudge against him, anyway?"

"Grudge?" Talbot echoed. "I don't have a grudge. I just don't like his type. Just like I don't like filthy redskins."

"The pastor's not hurting you any." Scott was watching Talbot closely. He stayed alert for movement among the ranks of Talbot's men. "Why don't you back off?"

"It's none of your concern, Colton."

"Sure it is," Scott said. "I don't want to lose my job."

"You keep siding with that preacher and you might lose your life."

"I wouldn't be alone in that case."

"Just don't forget what I say." Talbot's voice was hard. His face was ugly.

"I've got a real good memory," Scott said with equal menace.

Talbot glanced at Strike Foster. It was no more than a sideward flick of his eyes.

"You know what this is, Colton?" Foster lifted the throwing club.

"Your toy." Scott tried to keep his eyes on both men.

Casually Foster flicked his wrist. The club rose into the air in a lazy cartwheel. He caught it smoothly. "It's called a boomerang," he explained. "I got it down in Australia. I spent time there when things got hot for me here in some parts of the States. It's a danged funny place. They got animals you wouldn't believe, and there's whole tribes of savages that live kind of like the Indians over here. They use boomerangs to hunt with. They're like wizards with them. I've seen them do things with them that I'm not even sure I believe." He paused in his narrative and peeled his lips back from his teeth. Scott thought of a snake smiling. Foster went on:

"I had one of their craftsmen make me a special boomerang, heavier than the ones they use. I wanted to try it on heavier game." His smile was mirthless. "I practiced with it, and now I'm better than most of them. I can even kill a man with mine."

"Congratulations," Scott said. Involuntarily his hand had drifted to hover near his .45.

"You want a demonstration?" Foster asked softly.

"You're wasting drinking time, boys," a woman said.

Scott recognized the voice of Belle Tanner. He did not take his eyes off Foster, and Foster's never left him.

He had a peripheral impression of Talbot's head snapping around toward Belle.

Talbot shot a look at Foster. It was another command. Scott could see the killing tension ease slowly out of the gunman. He moved his own hand away from his .45. It had been a near thing there between him and Foster. Death had been close for one or both of them.

Slowly Scott turned his head. Belle Tanner stood in the middle of the street, hands on her hips. She wore an off-the-shoulder, dark red dress. It clung to her figure and was cut too low in front for modesty. A single large red stone gleamed against her flesh. A teasing smile played on her lips. Standing there, she dominated the entire crew of gunmen.

"Drinks are on the house, boys," she announced. Her teasing smile grew wider.

There was a stirring among the mounted men. Questioning glances were turned to Talbot. He stared hard at Belle for a long moment. She met his gaze boldly.

Abruptly Talbot jerked his head toward the Dark Lady. It was yet another nonverbal command. The horsemen swung their animals about toward the saloon across the street. In moments they had dismounted and were trooping through the batwing doors. Talbot spun the Appaloosa around harshly. His face was an expressionless mask. Foster threw a last hard look at Scott, then urged his horse after that of his boss.

Scott looked toward Belle Tanner. Her smile was roguish. "I still owe you a drink," she said before he could speak.

Scott hesitated. Just possibly, she had saved his life. He nodded his acceptance of the offer.

She waited for him and tucked her arm in his. "This way," she directed. "There's a back entrance. We'll avoid the riffraff."

They would also avoid Land Talbot, Scott reflected. It was probably just as well. She escorted him across the street and along the side of the saloon. Scott was extremely aware of her closeness, and of the heady scent she wore.

The back entrance led into a small foyer off the room where she had entertained him before. Scott guessed that her bedchamber was adjacent. It occurred to him that the foyer entrance made a convenient route for clandestine visitors.

A menacing gray shape seemed to take substance out of the air. Lobo snarled a ghostly silent warning. Scott felt his hackles rise like those of the wolf dog. Belle sent the beast slinking away with a word. Scott wondered why she had not taken Lobo with her to confront Talbot and his men. Surely she must have felt the need of a protector in those few moments.

"What will you have?" she asked from the bar.

Scott waved the decision back to her. She smiled knowingly, selected a bottle, and filled two shot glasses. He felt the tingling heat of her flesh as he took the glass from her. She sipped at her drink. Her tongue slipped across her crimson lips.

Scott tasted his own drink. It was good whiskey, he supposed, but he did not like to drink, because alcohol dulled the mind and slowed the reflexes, and either could be fatal when guns came into play. He set the glass back on the bar.

"Are you the peacekeeper around here?" he asked.

She brushed close past him as she went to settle once again on the chaise longue. Scott noted that Lobo was not in his customary place on its far side. "Gunfights in the street are bad for the town," she explained.

"Not to mention the people in them," Scott responded.

Her laughter rang clear. "That too," she agreed. "Come on and sit down." She brushed a hand across the chaise beside her.

Scott took the upholstered chair he had occupied before. He did not trust himself with this woman. And he did not trust her motives enough to let her tighten the seductive hold she already had on him. He liked to know the price of things before he had to pay it.

Her pouting smile held amusement as well. She slid across the chaise until she was close to him where he sat in the chair. "I also stepped in out there because I didn't want you hurt," she said huskily.

"Thanks."

"Foster's fast," she said, "even without his boomerang. And Talbot is almost as fast himself. That was a good part of his men with him."

"You handled them well," Scott commented.

"I told you, I'm good at reading men. I'm also good at handling them."

She seemed to have no interest in what had sparked the confrontation in the street. Maybe Talbot made a habit of rousting strangers in town. "Is Talbot a big man hereabouts?" Scott asked.

Her eyes grew serious. "It doesn't pay to cross him," she answered. "He usually gets what he wants."

The same could be said of her, Scott thought. "What does he want?" he asked.

Her eyes smoldered. "Me," she said boldly. "If I'd let him. But I won't."

"Smart decision."

"I wonder sometimes."

"What else does he want?"

She shrugged her bare shoulders. "Power, money. What do all men want?"

Scott thought of Brother Sam Prentiss. *Not all men,* he reflected. "What business is he in?" he asked.

She made a sound of stifled mirth. "The business of taking what he wants from whoever has it."

Her description of Talbot's occupation was not much different, in substance, from what Zeke Cantrell had told him. "What would Talbot have against Reverend Prentiss?"

"The preacher? Oh, that's right, you're working for him now, aren't you?"

"Just helping out."

"I told you that you had a job with me." She had ignored his earlier question.

"I'm not really working for him," Scott explained. "I'm just giving him and his kids a hand building their church."

"That daughter of his is hardly a kid." Her eyes regarded him shrewdly.

"She's a nice girl."

Belle appeared amused at his answer. "Why work for the good reverend if you're not getting paid?" She seemed to read some kind of answer in his eyes and leaned intently toward him. Scott felt the physical impact of her closeness. "You're wasting your time," she said with soft urgency. "You don't have any place with people like them. You and I are alike. We've lived on the edge for too long. When you do that, you fall over into the dark. Then there's no going back. Not ever."

Her attraction was suddenly overwhelming. He couldn't deny the truth of her words. He wanted to put his arms around her and crush her to him. He did not know what she would do if he tried.

"Work for me," she urged breathlessly. "Name your own terms."

What had he said about Ruth Prentiss only moments before? A nice girl, he had said. She was part of what a new beginning and a new life could offer him, while Belle Tanner, for all her seductive allure, was no more than a tempting and convenient way of rejecting that new life. The image of Ruth's warm smile hovered before his eyes.

"I don't think I can afford your wages," he said.

"No one's ever complained," she whispered.

"Your price is too high." Scott forced himself up out of the grasp of the chair.

Belle lay back on the chaise and gazed up at him with smoky eyes. She mirrored the pose in the painting behind her. "The offer still stands if you change your mind."

Scott nodded. He couldn't speak. He turned away from the beguiling sight of her and headed for the door. Lobo appeared at his heels like a ghost. The wolf dog stopped at the threshold as Scott let himself out through the back entrance.

His knees felt weak as he headed back across the

street. His mare had been moved from in front of the store, and now stood hitched at the adjacent stable. As he drew near, the lanky figure of Zeke appeared from within the barn.

"I moved your mare over here," he drawled. "I was fixing to put her up for you. I figured you'd be gone for a while." He gave Scott his customary up and down look. "I guess I figured wrong."

"Just barely," Scott admitted. He felt feverish and shaken.

Zeke shook his head. "Miss Belle's like that wolf of hers. Some men she'd as soon eat as look at. Fact is, I'm not sure how I'd choose between her and that wolf. Either way, you'd end up in pieces. One'd just be a little faster than the other. Course, I reckon she did save your life right out there."

"Could be," Scott conceded.

"She maybe thinks she owns a piece of you now. She has a piece of darn near everything else in town."

"Does she own as much of the town as she says?" The weakness was leaving Scott's legs.

"She owns a bunch. And I wouldn't be surprised if she has other holdings elsewhere."

"Why's that?"

"Seeing as how she's gone so much of the time. She's always riding off in her little fancy buggy or on horseback with that wolf right there alongside her. She stays gone for hours, even overnight sometimes. I figure she's going into Guthrie to look after whatever else she owns."

"Where did she get the money to buy that saloon?

Saving that much on what a bar girl makes wouldn't be easy."

Zeke shrugged. "Search me." He untied the sorrel's reins from the hitching rail and handed them to Scott. "I reckon you'll be headed back out to the church."

"Is everybody in town keeping track of me?" Scott asked wryly.

Zeke snorted. "You're big news, boy. Word's already around town that you shot up one of Talbot's boys, then whipped three more in a roughhouse to protect the preacher and his little girl. There's no telling what people will be saying after this episode just now."

Scott frowned. One of Talbot's men must have mentioned the incident with the Indian brave, Hunting Wolf. Talbot would not like having it spread around town that a stranger was working over his boys and getting away with it. "Real nice little town you've got here," he commented.

Zeke cackled. "You watch your back, boy. You picked a mean one to buck when you picked Talbot."

"I didn't pick him."

"Well, you've got him, and there's no backing out of it now, unless you tuck tail and run. Come to consider it, that might not be a bad move."

"Not yet," Scott said.

Zeke's look was shrewd. "Maybe never," he said. "You'll be staying out with the preacher and his clan, then?"

Scott thought of Talbot and Strike Foster. "We'll see," he answered.

Chapter Four

"Let us pray," Brother Sam said, bowing his head and clasping his workworn hands.

Before bowing his own head, Scott glanced about him at the Sunday-morning congregation. There were farm families with their gaggles of children, town women, a few merchants and cowhands, and even a pair of bar girls. Some of the cowhands, Scott noticed with relief, still wore their guns, just as he did.

In all, Scott estimated, some seventy-five people were present, and he was mildly surprised at the turnout. He wondered if it would have been even larger if not for Land Talbot's open and well-known animosity toward the church.

Brother Sam had seated the congregation on the grass in a small meadow beyond the church, where some of the construction lumber was stacked. He had been holding services there since his arrival in Meridian, Ruth had told Scott proudly. This particular morning the sky was a clear blue with soft clouds scudding

67

overhead. A cool breeze rippled the grass of the meadow. Tables had been set up for a potluck dinner following the service. It was an idyllic pastoral setting.

Brother Sam stood before his flock, Bible in hand. He wore a dark suit such as Scott had expected him to wear at dinner two nights ago. He radiated a strangely captivating presence as he began his opening prayer.

Belatedly Scott bowed his head. He sat on the outskirts of the crowd in the front rank. Even with his head bowed and his eyes closed, he was aware of Ruth's presence at his side. She had insisted that he sit there with her and Matt. Neither she nor the other members of her family had commented on the fact that he had come armed to church. He felt surprisingly at ease.

The prayer was a long one. Brother Sam's voice carried clearly. His sincerity was evident in his tone, Scott thought.

Next, Ruth rose from beside Scott and went forward as if on cue. There was a murmuring of anticipation in the crowd. Obviously Ruth took an active and familiar role in her father's services. She wore a plain white dress. Her golden hair was done up in a formal fashion, and she seemed to glow in the sunlight. She raised her face and eyes heavenward and began to sing in a pure, sweet voice.

Scott recognized the hymn: "Amazing Grace." He had not heard it in years. Its compelling, poignant words seemed to linger in the air when she finished. She sang another song, which was unfamiliar to Scott, and then she led the congregation in several more hymns.

As the voices faded on the final verse, Scott felt the first faint vibrations through the ground.

He jerked his head around. Now the sound of yells came to him with the drum of the hoofbeats he had sensed in the earth. A dozen racing horsemen swept out of the trees and into the midst of the congregation. The worshipers began to scatter as gunfire rang out.

Scott pulled his .45. He recognized the horsemen— Land Talbot and his gang. He swung his gun toward the nearest rider, but held his fire. The attackers were not shooting to kill. They were discharging their weapons into the air, he realized. If he fired on them, he would be inviting a bloodbath. Most of the worshipers were unarmed. They would have no chance if this became a gun battle.

Scott shoved the .45 back into its holster. The riders had completed one pass through the panicked crowd. Turning their horses, they came back. Women screamed. Men shouted in anger and fear. Everyone ran or staggered to get clear.

Scott glimpsed the ugly mask of Talbot's face. Talbot's Appaloosa loomed over him. Beside Talbot was Strike Foster, his mouth pulled back in his snake's grin. He flailed at Scott's head with the boomerang as he raced past. Scott ducked away. He felt the rush of air by his head.

Frantically he looked for Ruth. Her white dress stood out. Instead of staying clear of the action, she had rushed forward to help or defend. She knelt protectively by a small crying boy. A bearded man on a roan horse bore down upon her. Scott heard his drunken yell of surprise. The roan was out of his control. It was running wild. Ruth and the child were directly in its path.

Scott dashed toward her. A man stumbled against him. He fended him off. He did not know or care who it was. He flung himself the last few yards in a straining dive. He felt the softness of Ruth's form in the moment of collision. His arms encircled her and the child. The force of his lunge sent them rolling across the grass. He locked his grip tight. The hooves of the horse pounded past them. The rider yelled wildly again.

Scott scrambled to his feet and pulled up Ruth and the child. The boy was crying loudly. Ruth looked shaken. "Get him clear!" Scott yelled. "Into the woods!"

Ruth grabbed the child's hand and dragged him toward the protection of the trees. Guns or no, Scott thought, the roust had turned dangerous.

And it was not over. He saw a horseman try to jump his mount over one of the picnic tables. He didn't make it. The horse's rear hooves clipped the table and toppled it. The horse barely stayed on its feet as it came down. The rider was nearly jolted from his saddle.

Another rider came at Scott. *All right,* he thought, *no guns.* He sidestepped the rush of the horse. As it swept on past, he sprang at the rider like a leaping cat. His hands gripped the man's shirt. He hauled the man from the horse and slammed him hard to the ground. The raider floundered, gasping for air. Scott booted him behind the ear to put him out.

The pile of lumber was nearby. Scott snatched a two-by-four from it. He felt the splinters bite into his palms. He whirled with it and swung at another raider with everything he had in his shoulders. The board splintered across the rider's chest. The impact bowled the fellow backward out of his saddle. Scott was spun about. Somehow the edge of the two-by-four caught him jarringly along the side of his head. He reeled and fell to his knees.

For a while the shouts and the gunfire and the pounding of hooves faded from him. When they swelled back, they seemed strangely muted. He blinked against a painful brightness.

He saw one of the men he had felled being pulled up behind another rider. There was no sign of his other victim. The remaining riders were racing away. Parting yells and a few gunshots drifted back in their wake.

Scott pushed himself to his feet. Automatically he checked his .45. It remained in its holster. He should have used it, he thought bitterly. The freak impact of the two-by-four had momentarily stunned him. The attackers had ridden out.

He tried to take stock. People were milling about uncertainly. No one appeared to be seriously injured, but there would be plenty of scrapes and bruises. Talbot had not said anything to him during the attack, but the message to both Scott and the Prentiss family was clear. Scott felt a surge of baffled anger.

Ruth ran toward him. She checked herself at the last moment and pulled up short. "Are you all right?" she panted.

Scott nodded. His headache was already fading. "You?" he asked.

"I'm all right." She nodded as if the subject was unimportant. "I had to take care of that little boy. And then I saw you'd been hurt. . . ." She let it trail off. Her eyes were bright with moisture.

Scott resisted the impulse to reach out and hug her to him. He felt a curious thrill at her concern for him. "I'm fine," he told her.

"Oh, they're starting to leave!" she cried. Something behind him had caught her attention.

Scott looked around. Several families were heading toward their wagons.

"Brothers! Sisters!" The voice of Sam Prentiss rang across the meadow. Scott saw that the pastor had mounted one of the remaining picnic tables. His suit was disheveled, but he made a commanding figure. Movement in the meadow stilled. He called out:

"Let us not allow the actions of these pagans to prevent us from worshiping the Lord! Come! Return to your places! Our service is not yet over."

One of the cowhands moved first. Casually he ambled back over to the area where the congregation had been sitting. Next a farmer led his family. Gradually the rest of the people followed suit.

Ruth turned a joyful glance on Scott. Her face was radiant.

"Good sermon, preacher," the gnarled farmer said.

Brother Sam gripped his hand warmly and murmured thanks. The farmer led his wife and five children toward their wagon. The other members of the congregation were also dispersing. Some of them headed back to town. Most, like the farmer, turned their animals toward the range. Brother Sam watched them go with satisfaction.

The service and communal meal had been a success despite the disruption by Land Talbot and his gang. In fact, the raid had strengthened the spirit of the service. Scott pondered about it as he stood with Brother Sam and his children, watching the worshipers leave.

"I didn't think Talbot would go this far," Brother Sam said wearily. Some of the strength seemed to fade from him. "We may have trouble attracting a congregation after this."

"People will still come," Ruth said. "Not everyone's scared of Talbot."

"Scott tried to stop them," Matt said with pride. "Why didn't you use your gun, Scott?"

"They weren't trying to kill anybody. I didn't want to be the one to start."

"That was wise," Brother Sam said. "You probably avoided a massacre."

"You knocked two of them off their horses," Matt went on with excitement. "I tried to do it with one man, but he kicked me away." His forehead bore a darkening bruise. "How did you know how to do that, Scott?"

"I've done it before." Scott sighed. Actually, he was not too pleased with himself. He had unseated two of the riders, but had managed to almost knock himself unconscious in the process. It was not a performance he was proud of. He felt the eyes of Ruth and Sam on him as he told Matt, "In the long run, knowing how to use a hammer and how to build are better skills than knowing how to take a man off a horse." *Or how to shoot a man down,* he added silently.

Matt was thoughtful for a while. "I guess that's right," he agreed at last.

"I appreciate your standing with us," Brother Sam told Scott. "You didn't have to try to help."

"Yes, I did," Scott said.

The pastor studied him a moment, then nodded sagely. "Perhaps you did, at that."

"Let's go back to camp," Ruth suggested. She stayed near Scott as they returned.

"Maybe Talbot will give up when he sees we aren't scared of him," Matt said. "Maybe he won't try anything else."

"He already has tried something else," Scott informed them.

"What do you mean?" Ruth asked quickly.

Scott told them about his conversation with the storekeeper in Meridian the day before.

"But why?" Ruth questioned. "Father always pays his bills."

"I think the storekeeper's scared of Talbot," Scott explained. "A lot of the townspeople are. Talbot might've told him to freeze your credit."

"That sounds too subtle for Talbot," the pastor commented. But the news distressed him. He was frowning moodily as they settled back at the camp. "Ruth, Matt," he addressed his children, "I think this situation is going to get worse before it gets better. I won't let Talbot drive me off, not when I know I'm where I'm supposed to be and doing what I'm supposed to be doing. But it's too dangerous for you to stay out here. I want both of you to move back to town today."

"No!" Matt yelled angrily. "I'm not leaving you out here by yourself! I can help do whatever needs to be done!"

"I'm not leaving, either," Ruth told him firmly. She moved closer to Matt so they presented a united front. "We're all part of this family. If you're supposed to be here, then so are we."

Brother Sam gauged the determination in their stiff stances. "Ruth," he appealed, "it's dangerous for you to be out here."

"It's just as dangerous for you, Father. Things might get worse before they get better, but they *will* get better. I know they will! And you can't just send me off to town because there might be danger out here. Why do you think I'd be any safer in town, alone or with Matt, than I would be here with you? Have you forgotten what happened the last time we went to town? Scott had to help us fight off those bullies."

Brother Sam shook his head in resignation, but Scott detected pride in the look he gave his children. He turned to Scott.

"That leaves you, Scott. Like I told you, I appreciate all you've done for us, but I can't ask you to go on fighting our battles for us."

"Maybe I'm fighting my own battles too," Scott said. He felt Ruth's eyes fix on him intently, and he groped for words. "I've spent almost half my life fighting for the wrong things. I'm through with that now. I want to put it behind me. Maybe it's time I started fighting for the right things."

Brother Sam drew a deep breath. "I guess you'll need to stay out here, then," he told Scott. "I can't pay you anything, though."

"I'll give you a line of credit," Scott said, grinning.

"I left a few things in the hotel in town. I need to go back and get them. I'll do that now."

"Today is Sunday," Brother Sam said. "It's a day of rest. Tomorrow we'll start work on the church again."

Scott saddled the sorrel. He felt a peaceful contentment within him. He had taken a stand. Like Brother Sam, he was sure he was doing the right thing. He let the sorrel have her head, and she hit an exhilarating gallop into town.

Things were quiet in Meridian on Sunday afternoon. A few loafers still hung around the saloons. He saw no sign of Zeke as he passed the stable. At the rooming house he checked out and then mounted the stairs to pick up his meager belongings. Inside his room he collected them—a few changes of clothing, an old Colt .44 Dragoon revolver, a hunting knife, a trail kit, and a couple of dime novels. It was not much to show for twenty-five years of life, he reflected.

He had it all bundled under his arm when there was a knock on the door. Scott stepped clear and drew his .45. He reached out and pulled the door open. Belle Tanner smiled mockingly when she saw the .45.

"Expecting company?" she asked. Lobo was at her side. The wolf dog stood taller than her waist. He, too, seemed to see and understand the potential of the gun. His snarl was a savage, gurgling rumble.

Scott resisted the urge to step back and level his gun at the animal. He remembered Zeke's telling him that Lobo was a man killer.

Belle's dark eyes glittered. "Lobo." The word stilled the animal. Her tongue slid over her lips. "Stay. Guard." She stepped past Scott and into the room. She pushed the door shut on Lobo's yellow eyes. She turned to face Scott. "He won't let us be disturbed."

Scott didn't doubt it. He hoped that none of the hostelry's other occupants stepped into the hallway. He slid the .45 back into its holster. He looked at her and felt the physical impact of her beauty.

She wore an elegant blue dress that would have been appropriate in the finest of cosmopolitan settings. She struck a pose as if for an artist. Scott realized she was basking in his admiration.

"I was just leaving," he told her.

"Going back to the preacher?" she inquired with an undertone of malice.

"That's right."

She made a graceful turn like a performer displaying her beauty on stage before an admiring audience. "I heard his morning service didn't go well."

"No one left until it was over."

She did not seem to hear his answer. She inclined her head slightly to one side. "My offer's still open, you know."

"I don't think my answer has changed."

"Are you sure you're not making a mistake?"

He shrugged. "If I went to work for you, I wouldn't be sure, either."

She considered his reply. "If I were you, I'd give it some thought. Land doesn't want that church built."

"Maybe that's a good reason to build it."

"It's dangerous to buck Land Talbot in this town."

"Lady, it's dangerous to go to church in this town."

She made an impatient gesture of dismissal. "You don't belong in church or nursemaiding a do-good preacher and his children. You're a fighting man. I know your type. I've seen them in bars all over the Territory. They come and go every day in the Dark Lady. Gunfighters and killers. You don't know anything beyond the gun. You're at your best when you have a gun in your fist and you're betting your life that you're better with that gun than anyone else who lives by the same rules."

Scott thought of Talbot's man whom he had wounded rather than killed, of his reluctance to start a gunfight where innocent lives would be lost, and of his commitment to stand by Samuel Prentiss and his cause. "Maybe once," he answered her. "Not anymore."

Anger, or passion, or maybe both, flared in her dark eyes. But when she spoke, her voice was calm. "Then you won't reconsider?"

"I already have. The answer's still no."

"I hope you live long enough to regret it!"

Scott had to step aside as she swept past him and out the door.

Chapter Five

"Scott, I've got some legal papers that need to be filed in Guthrie," Brother Sam said. "They have to do with our title to this land. I've neglected to file them before now, but with all the problems we're having, I want to make absolutely sure that there's no way our right to the property can be legally contested. Would you be able to take them into Guthrie tomorrow?"

"Sure," Scott agreed.

"May I go with him, Father?"

Brother Sam looked at his daughter. He had just emerged from the tent and was approaching the campfire where the three young people sat in the gathering darkness.

"Please," Ruth implored. "I'll be all right. Scott can take care of me. I've been wanting to see Guthrie again. We never got much of a chance to look around when we came through before. And I need some material to make a new dress for when we officially open the church. If I don't get started on it pretty soon, I won't have it finished in time." She fixed an eager, expectant gaze on her father.

Scott found himself holding his breath as he awaited the reply.

"I suppose it would be all right," Brother Sam conceded. "But I want you back by dark."

"I can get my fabric while Scott's filing the papers," Ruth assured him. She turned eagerly to Scott. "I'll fix us a picnic lunch!"

Her enthusiasm was contagious, and Scott became excited at the prospect of their excursion. "You and Matt keep an eye out for trouble while we're gone," he advised Brother Sam.

"We'll be careful. Things have been quiet for a couple of days now."

"That doesn't mean it's over."

Sam was right, though, Scott reflected. In the two days since the disrupted service on Sunday, there had been no further evidence of hostilities from Talbot. Work on the church had proceeded at a rapid pace.

"I'll get started on our lunch now!" Ruth bounced to her feet and hurried toward the tent.

Brother Sam gave Scott a long, probing look.

"I'll take care of her," Scott said.

"I know you will." Brother Sam grinned. "Do you think I'd let her go with you, otherwise?"

Busy with the demanding work of building the church, Scott had had little time to spend with Ruth, but her cheerful presence had become a familiar and welcome aspect of his days. His anticipation of a day spent with her stayed with him as he bedded down. His sleep was light, and he was up early to hitch the horses to the wagon.

"Here's our lunch." Ruth came staggering up with a heavy basket. "I fixed all kinds of things—ham and greens and bread and sugar cookies."

"It sounds good." Scott took the basket from her, their hands brushing. He hefted the basket into the wagon and turned back to meet her grin with one of his own.

"Hey, you two," Matt's voice sounded from nearby. "No stopping under a tree somewhere to spark."

"Oh, Matt, you hush!" Ruth scolded him. "I've got to finish breakfast." She cast a last fetching smile at Scott.

As he busied himself with the horses, he was conscious of Matt's approach. "You like Sis, don't you?" the youth asked after a moment.

"Yeah, I sure do," Scott told him honestly. He still felt a tingling sense of surprise whenever he paused to reflect on the growing depth of his feelings for the preacher's daughter, as well as the fact that she had not spurned his attentions outright.

"I'm glad," Matt said. He turned and walked away before Scott could answer.

They set out after breakfast. Brother Sam called a cheerful farewell after them. Beside Scott, Ruth twisted around in the wagon seat to wave back at him. Scott smelled the sweet lilac scent she wore. Her face was framed by a blue sunbonnet. Beneath its shade, her eyes sparkled with little lights that made Scott smile, and he found himself comparing her clean freshness with the gilded sophistication of Belle Tanner. The thought of the saloon owner left him cold.

Scott bypassed Meridian and headed west, where Guthrie lay some ten miles distant. Ruth chattered happily as the wagon creaked over the rolling prairie. Scott enjoyed the sound of her voice. She was excited at the prospect of their journey.

"Oh, look!" She pointed at the herd of pronghorn antelope that flashed away across the grassland. Scott caught himself looking at her laughing smile rather than the fleet animals. Turning her head, she caught him gazing at her. A blush rushed over her face, but she didn't seem displeased.

As they neared Guthrie they encountered more traffic. A medicine dealer's gaudy wagon went past them, headed for town. It was pulled by a team of mules, and the slick-haired dealer eyed them shrewdly as he passed. Evidently he had decided that they were poor prospects for his wares. He urged on the plodding mules with a popping whip.

A pair of cowhands hazed a small herd of cattle along the side of the road. They shouted at Ruth with good-natured exuberance. Scott waved back at them.

As they rolled into town, the dirt track gave way to cobblestoned streets. Business and enterprise seemed to be booming in the territorial capital. Traffic was heavy, and pedestrians and horsemen vied for space with carriages and wagons.

"I just love it here," Ruth said, exhilarated. "When I learned we were going to Oklahoma Territory, I read all about Guthrie. Look at the beautiful buildings. Almost all of them were designed by Joseph Foucart. He's a European architect who came to this city and liked it so much he stayed."

Scott noted the elaborate turrets, arched windows, and scrolled tinwork adorning many of the buildings. Guthrie, he recalled, had been designed from its inception to serve as the capital. Its architecture and refinements rivaled the nation's most cosmopolitan cities.

"They even have electric lights here, and indoor plumbing." Ruth confirmed his thoughts. "There's a tunnel system connecting most of the buildings."

Scott noted a bank on the ground floor of a building. Lodging rooms were rented on the second floor. They passed the notorious Blue Belle Saloon and the hotel adjacent to it. Not very many years before, this had all been open prairie, Scott reflected with wonder.

He asked a graying U.S. deputy marshal for directions. Ruth spotted a dry-goods store where she could purchase fabric. Scott let her off at its door with a promise to return within an hour. It took him most of that time to arrange for the filing of the legal papers. The clerks at the courthouse appeared harried and overworked in their task of keeping track of the numerous records.

He negotiated the wagon back along the crowded streets to the dry-goods store. Ruth met him on the boardwalk with a package of fabric. She refused to let him see the pattern. "You'll see it when I've finished the dress," she promised. Her face was flushed with excitement as she took in the colorful sights. "Can we look around some before we go?" she asked eagerly.

Scott offered his arm. It felt good to be strolling with this girl amidst the bustle of activity. She exclaimed at various exhibits in the windows of the shops. Willingly he let himself be dragged from one display to the next.

"Isn't that beautiful?" She was staring wide-eyed at a shimmering yellow silk dress on a mannequin.

"Yours will be prettier when you get it made," Scott told her.

She tightened her grip on his arm. "Silly," she chided. But he could tell she was pleased.

He bought cold sodas at a pharmacy. They found an entrance to the tunnel system and, sipping their drinks, they wandered through the paved and lighted underground walkways.

"I'm getting hungry for our lunch," Scott hinted.

She did not protest, and they headed back to the wagon.

She glanced around one last time as they were leaving town. Then she turned her attention to Scott. "That was fun."

Scott grinned at her. "Maybe we can go back again sometime," he said.

"Okay!" she accepted quickly.

Scott's heart was beating faster. He jiggled the reins unnecessarily to keep the horses moving.

He spotted a copse of trees a quarter mile off the road and turned toward it. In the cool shade beneath the trees he halted the team. Ruth unfolded a blanket and spread it on the ground. She unpacked their lunch, shooing Scott off when he tried awkwardly to help.

"Now," she announced at last. "We can say grace and eat." She murmured a quick prayer for them both, then passed ham and bread and greens to Scott.

Scott found himself relaxing. Birds sang cheerfully.

A faint breeze from the prairie brushed through the trees. Ruth took off her bonnet and sat beside him as they ate.

Scott finished first, and then turned his head and watched her silently. After a few moments she turned toward him with a hesitant, questioning smile. Scott slid his arm around her shoulders and leaned over to kiss her. Her lips were warm and responsive to his. He drew back after a time and met the soft gaze of her brown eyes.

"I don't know very much about you," she whispered.

Scott looked away. She had a right to know, and he wanted her to know. Staring into the trees, he began to talk, telling her of being raised by an uncaring farmer after the deaths of his parents from pneumonia when he was only a boy. The farmer had wanted a slave, not a son. As he spoke, Scott seemed to feel once again the pain of the overwork and the frequent beatings. When he looked at Ruth, he read a tender sympathy in her eyes.

"I ran away when I was twelve." He looked back into the branches. "I fell in with a bounty man. He taught me how to use a gun before he was killed by a bank robber we were tracking. I killed the bank robber and collected the bounty. I knew I was good with a gun from the very beginning. I didn't know any other trade. I had some choices as to how to use what I knew. I could keep on hunting down wanted men for the prices on their heads, or I could hire out my gun to the highest bidder, or I could go outside the law myself. I wouldn't do the last one, but I never saw much wrong with either of the first two choices."

"Why did you quit?" Ruth asked softly. She placed a warm hand on his. He gripped it tightly.

"Too many victims. Too many faces I remembered in front of my gun. Most were wanted men, or others, like me, who were willing to gamble for their pay that they were better with a gun than anyone the other side could hire. I never found anybody better than me. But it got to where no matter what I was paid, or how high the bounty was, it didn't seem enough. Finally I realized that I was selling more than my gun. I was selling my spirit as well. I had to quit." He knew his uncertainties must be evident on his face. Her hand was returning the pressure of his.

"You've quit that life," she said with soft urgency. "You can put it behind you now. I'll help you."

Wordlessly Scott took her in his arms and hugged her tightly to him. He felt her arms around him.

"We'd better be going," he said huskily after a long moment. Reluctantly he released her.

She nodded without speaking, and began to collect their leftovers.

"I love you," Scott said. He had not intended to speak.

She swung her head around to face him. Her eyes filled with tears. Her smile was joyful. "I love you too," she whispered.

This time their kiss was longer. When they left the grove, she sat close beside him on the wagon seat. Scott kept wanting to stare into her eyes. He had to pull his gaze away and force himself to scan the prairie for possible danger.

She giggled.

"What's that for?" he asked in confusion.

"I was just thinking. We did exactly what Matt told us not to do. We stopped under a tree to spark."

Scott laughed too.

He was still smiling when he saw the group of figures walking in the road ahead. The party shifted aside as he approached. He saw flat copper faces and clothing ranging from buckskins to store-bought work clothes. One of the figures stepped suddenly forward, lifting a hand in recognition.

Scott pulled the team to a halt. "Hunting Wolf," he said in greeting.

"I remember you, Scott Colton," the brave said formally.

"It's good to see you," Scott responded.

Hunting Wolf gestured at his companions. "We have come from town."

There were four men and two women, one of them with child. A gaunt paint pony pulled a loaded travois. The men carried bows or ancient firearms. Obviously they had been to Guthrie to purchase supplies. The territorial capital was probably safer for them than Meridian, where Land Talbot's influence was felt. They had a long walk ahead of them, Scott reflected.

"I hope your people are well," Scott told him.

Hunting Wolf nodded solemnly. He wore buckskin leggings and a beaded vest rather than the white man's clothes of some of his companions. He carried both a bow and a battered old Winchester. "We are well. We are careful to stay in groups since you shoot white gunman to save me. I tell my people of what you do. They not forget." Scott felt the dark, unreadable eyes of the other Indians on him. "We see no more of those white men."

"I am glad," Scott told him. He hoped Talbot would continue to leave the Indians alone, but he felt certain that Hunting Wolf and his people would never be completely safe from the hostility of Talbot and men like him.

Hunting Wolf turned his gaze on Ruth. "This your woman?" he asked.

"Yes," Scott answered proudly.

Again came the solemn nod. "She daughter of white preacher man building church in Meridian," he stated. "We see them work. They good people. Preacher man once talk to some of my people on road. They listen to his words."

"I am helping them build the church," Scott told him.

"That good. You wear gun like men who hunt me, but I see in your eyes that you different." Hunting Wolf turned and indicated the young woman with child. She was pretty. "This my woman," Hunting Wolf announced proudly. "She Running Doe. Soon she give me son." Modestly, the young woman lowered her eyes from their gazes.

"Your son will be a strong man, like his father," Scott predicted.

Hunting Wolf grunted in acknowledgment of the compliment. "You bring your woman, her family, visit my people." He swept an arm off to the northeast.

"Thank you. Your offer is gracious." Scott added, "Our wagon is large. We can take you to your village so you will not have to walk."

Hunting Wolf shook his head. "We walk," he stated firmly. But he seemed pleased by the offer. Without further words he turned and strode away. His companions followed. Running Doe glanced back at Ruth and smiled.

They watched the Indians depart. The party headed north and east from the road between Guthrie and Meridian. Scott hoped that they made it to their village without incident.

"He mentioned that you shot a man," Ruth said a few minutes later.

Scott nodded, then told her of his earlier encounter with Hunting Wolf and Land Talbot.

"That's wonderful!" she cried when he finished. "You saved his life!"

"I had to shoot a man to do it."

"But you didn't kill him when you could have." She laid a hand on his arm. "You were fighting for the right things. You shouldn't condemn yourself for that."

Scott didn't answer, but her words relieved him of much of the pressure bearing down on his conscience. He jiggled the reins to move the horses forward. They were passing across rolling grassland striped with occasional lines of trees, and with undergrowth flanking the courses of meandering creeks. Rugged outcroppings of massive rocks thrust forth from some of the hilltops.

As they skirted the base of a long hill on their left, Scott caught a flicker of motion among the rocks at the hill's summit. The instincts of the gunman were still with him, and he turned his head sharply to look in that direction. The bullet went past his cheek so close that its heat seared his flesh. The sound of the shot was simultaneous. Scott wrapped his arms around Ruth and leaped out of the wagon seat in a desperate lunging dive. In midair he wiped the .45 clear of leather. Turning his head had saved him. The bullet had been meant to split his skull.

He twisted to take the impact of their landing on his side and shoulder, shielding Ruth. The wagon was between them and the dry-gulcher atop the hill. The horses had not bolted. They had stopped as the reins went slack.

Scott's gun was in his hand, and he came to his feet, using his left hand to keep Ruth down. He reached to put on the wagon's brake so that the horses couldn't bolt off. Another shot chewed splinters of wood from the side of the wagon by his head. He ducked low.

Crouching, he moved swiftly to the other end of the wagon. He straightened and fired three shots at the rock outcropping. He grabbed his Winchester from the bed of the wagon and ducked back under cover. Another shot snapped past overhead. Whoever was shooting was using a rifle.

The range was too great for accuracy with the .45. He replaced the spent shells as he surveyed the terrain. A creek wandered past some twenty yards behind them. Trees and growth cloaked its banks. He looked back toward the rocks sheltering their enemy. There was no cover available between their position and the rocks at the crest of the hill.

"Can you use this?" He showed Ruth the .45.

Her features were strained, but she was in control of herself. She shook her head at his question. "Father taught me how to use a saddle gun, though."

He would have preferred for her to have the .45, but he handed her the rifle. "Put a shot up there occasionally to keep his attention," he ordered. "Move back and forth behind the wagon and fire from different points so he won't know where to aim next. Don't give him a pattern to anticipate." Tight-lipped, she nodded. "I'm going into that creek bed behind us," Scott went on. "I'll see if I can use it for cover until I can outflank him. Then I'll try to move up that hill and get close enough for a shot."

"Be careful." Expertly she jacked a shell into the Winchester.

Scott remembered what she had said about fighting for the right things. She was ready to fight for them too. "Now," he told her. He dropped to his belly and snaked his way through the tall grass toward the shelter of the trees along the creek.

Behind him he heard her fire. A shot from their ambusher answered. He looked back sharply. She was unhurt, crouching to lever another shell into the chamber. He did not look back again. He hated to leave her exchanging shots with their enemy, but his plan offered their best chance of turning the tables on the drygulcher.

He made it into the cover of the underbrush and slid down the steep bank to the creek. No shots followed him. He did not think he had been seen. He heard Ruth fire again. The lip of the creek bed was higher than his head. He ran along the creek bed, splashing through water at times. He scrambled over a deadfall of brush and tree trunks. He fretted at the delay. To his rear, the shots continued in counterpoint, and he muttered a prayer for Ruth's safety.

When he thought he had gone far enough, he clawed his way up the bank until he could peer over the edge. He was muddy and panting. Through the brush he could see the hill. The wagon was back to his left. A shot rang out from Ruth's position there.

Scott pulled himself on up over the edge of the bank. From the edge of the brush he studied the lay of the terrain. He did not want to take the time to work his way to the rocks under the inadequate cover of the waving grass. Emerging from cover, he ran toward the hill, gun in hand.

It was a good hundred yards, part of it uphill. He did not slow down, because the longer he was in the open, the more likely he was to be seen. He reached the foot of the hill and started to climb it. He would be approaching the dry-gulcher from the flank. His lungs strained for breath.

Halfway up the hill's slope, he detected movement in the rocks, then glimpsed a silhouetted figure swinging a rifle toward him. He flung himself flat and fired three shots. He thought he saw the figure jolted backward. He rolled to his right and came back up to his feet. He charged the rest of the way with a panting cry of attack.

Three shots were left in his gun. He reached the rocks and plunged in among them. There was no one. Cartridge cases glittered on the ground. Across the grassland he saw a mounted rider headed away at a dead run. The range was too great, but he emptied the .45 after the rider.

He lowered the empty Colt and stood staring after the fleeing figure. His nerve broken by Scott's charge, the dry-gulcher had taken to his heels. There was no chance of catching him. Wearily, Scott started back down the hill to Ruth, who was running to meet him.

Chapter Six

"I've been wanting an opportunity to visit the Indian village," Brother Sam said with satisfaction. "Maybe this will provide one. You say this brave, Hunting Wolf, definitely included all of us in his invitation?"

"That's right," Ruth told him. "I think it would be wonderful to go. Don't you, Scott?"

Scott found it hard to resist her enthusiasm. "Sure," he agreed.

Brother Sam looked back and forth between them. His gaze was piercing. He and Matt had listened with interest to Ruth's telling of the encounter with the Indians and the dry-gulcher that afternoon. After assurances that his daughter and Scott were unharmed, he had broached the subject of a visit to the Indian village.

"Is tomorrow too early to go?" he asked now. "I think our work on the church could wait for a day. It's in a good cause."

There were no dissents. Matt grinned with excited

anticipation. "There's a ministry to be had among the Indian people," Brother Sam said thoughtfully. "I've always believed that. I've known other men of the cloth to turn away from trying to reach the Indians, but they, too, have spiritual needs that the church must minister to. Maybe this will give me a chance to start doing that."

Scott left Ruth to further describe their excursion to Guthrie, and he set about unhitching the horses from the wagon. His eye fell on the white scar in the wood where the dry-gulcher's shot had almost taken him down.

"You couldn't identify the attacker?" Brother Sam said as he approached. Ruth still chattered to Matt near the tent.

Scott shook his head. "He got clear, but I'm sure I hit him."

"Do you think it was one of Talbot's men?"

"Either one of his men or a robber who just happened to pick us out. But he seemed too persistent for a robber." Scott considered a moment. "It doesn't feel like Talbot's style."

"No, it doesn't," Sam agreed.

"At any rate, we need to keep our eyes open and watch our backs. I think you and I and Matt should take turns standing guard here at night."

"Perhaps you're right." Brother Sam glanced back over his shoulder at his children. "Ruth will want to take her turn too."

Scott recalled her competent handling of the Winchester. "All right. We'll go over some rules after dinner."

Brother Sam's gaze was intent. "Thank you for taking care of Ruth today."

"She did her part," Scott protested.

"You know what I mean."

After a moment Scott nodded. "I won't let anything happen to her."

Hunting Wolf's village was an odd collection of frame homes mixed with traditional domed grass houses and earthen lodges. It was at the foot of a sloping hill near a stream. Women moved about, engaged in various tasks. Some older children assisted them. The younger ones played nearby. Beyond the village were cultivated fields where men worked.

Scott sat his sorrel mare beside the Prentiss wagon atop one of the hills and surveyed the village. He saw the hanging bodies of deer and antelope, which the hunters had brought home, and he saw women grinding corn. The village, with its odd mixture of structures and activities, illustrated poignantly the disrupting pressures to which the Indian culture was being subjected.

Scott was not sure that the village had any legal status, because it was not on reservation land. He guessed that one of the members of the tribe might have exercised his right to claim land during the land run, and then allowed the rest of the tribe to settle on his land. They appeared to survive by a combination of traditional hunting, white men's farming techniques, and trade with the merchants in Guthrie.

The sun was well up in the sky. The time spent in travel and in locating the village had consumed much of the morning. Scott glanced over to Brother Sam at

the reins of the wagon. Both the pastor and his children
were studying the village with interest. Scott started the
sorrel down the slope.

They had been seen. Activity in the village stopped
and men began to come in from the fields. Scott spotted
Hunting Wolf among them. The brave came striding
to meet them as they rode into the village. A smile split
his usually rigid features. Others of the tribe crowded
up behind him to greet the newcomers. Hunting Wolf's
wife, Running Doe, smiled warmly at Ruth.

"We eat noon meal," Hunting Wolf announced once
he had gripped hands with the three white males. "You
our guests. Women fix meal now." Apparently the
young warrior was a man of authority in the village,
because Running Doe and several other women immediately headed toward the mismatched collection of
homes and lodges.

"I'll help them," Ruth offered, looking to her father
for permission. Her excitement and fascination with the
Indian village were evident. Brother Sam nodded his
approval, and she hurried after the women. Glancing
back, Running Doe saw her and waited. The two began
to converse with words and gestures.

The meal consisted of venison, fried bread, and
greens. Ruth helped the Indian women serve it, then
retired with them to eat separately. There was much
smiling and giggling between her and Running Doe.
The two young women cast frequent glances at Scott
and Hunting Wolf. Scott wondered if the brave felt as
self-conscious as he did.

"I would like to speak to your people," Brother Sam

requested once the meal was finished. The dozen or so men were seated in a ragged circle.

"Some maybe listen now," Hunting Wolf responded. "You come evening, all listen."

Brother Sam nodded. "I understand."

"*We* listen now," an older warrior spoke up. He gestured toward two other older men, who nodded gravely.

The other braves had begun to drift back to whatever jobs had occupied them. Most, Scott saw, were returning to the fields. A young man of about Matt's age was busy showing him a hunting knife and a bow.

Together with Hunting Wolf, Scott strolled away from Brother Sam and his small audience. They ascended the hill above the village.

Scott glanced at his companion. "Your people are kind," he said.

Hunting Wolf's voice carried a yearning sadness. "My people have little left. We not try fight white man anymore. Some try live by the old ways, but that no good now. Others try live white man's way. That maybe work, but it not good for my people." He waved an arm at the village below. "We lose old ways, but not able to live white man's way."

Scott looked down at the village. He estimated that it consisted of no more than ten families. Their tribal characteristics and heritage were rapidly being eroded by the crush and encroachment of white men and their society. He wondered if one day the Indians, like the buffalo herds of old, might virtually vanish from the West.

"You good man," Hunting Wolf said. "Preacher

good man too. We no want fight good men. Your woman and mine now friends. You and me friends too."

Scott nodded. "We are friends," he confirmed. It was all he had to offer this proud man. It did not seem enough.

Hunting Wolf looked past him and out across the range. Scott saw his gauntly muscled form stiffen. "Men come!" the brave said sharply.

Scott looked in the direction of his gaze and saw the mounted men who were approaching the village. He counted fifteen of them. The nearest was still out of rifle range, but they were coming fast. Scott felt a chill that was part fear and part cold anticipation. Even at that distance he could recognize the arrogant figure on the big Appaloosa. Land Talbot was at the center of his closing arc of men.

Hunting Wolf grunted wordlessly. Scott knew that the warrior had also recognized Talbot.

"Get back to the village," Scott said crisply. "Get your men under cover and ready to fight." He pulled the .45. "I'll slow them down and give you time."

He did not for a moment doubt Talbot's intentions. Thwarted by Scott in his earlier deadly game with Hunting Wolf, Talbot was leading his men on a raid of the village to vent his hatred of the Indians. This would be no simple ride-through harassment as had been the case during the church service. Against the Indians, with their questionable legal status, Talbot would have no qualms in ordering his men to kill, and the inhabitants of the village would be slaughtered.

Scott lifted the .45. He steadied his gun hand in the

palm of his other hand. It was a stance he had developed through trial and error for long-distance shooting. He sighted on the figure nearest to him at the far right end of the arc. He drew a deep breath.

The range was still ridiculous for a handgun, but he had no time to rush to the village for his Winchester. The raiders would be upon them before he could return to this site. The .45 was his only chance. The distance, the wind, and the movement of his target were all factors that could affect his aim. The first shot would probably do no more than warn them of his presence. The odds against his hitting his target were great, but with each successive shot, as his target came closer into range, those odds would be reduced.

Scott thumbed back the hammer of the .45. He sighted on the distant figure and squeezed the trigger. The .45 bucked and roared in his hands. He thumbed the hammer back and fired again, then again. He emptied the .45 at that single far-off target.

On the sixth shot the distant rider abruptly jerked his horse so that it swerved out of line. The animal went a few steps, then halted. The rider remained mounted. A hit, Scott thought. Probably not a kill at this distance, but a hit nonetheless. Talbot's fighting force had been reduced by one.

The arc was faltering now as the riders realized they were under fire. Scott heard a faint voice bawling orders. It was Talbot. After a moment the arc of riders swept on toward the village at a run.

Scott turned and raced down the hill. He reloaded as he ran. Hunting Wolf was busy trying to organize the inhabitants of the village for defense. Scott spotted

Ruth still with the Indian women. One of the men was ushering them into the sanctuary of an earthen lodge. Ruth threw Scott a look of questioning dismay. He waved at her to accompany the women. Frowning, she obeyed.

Matt and his father came running. "What is it?" Matt demanded.

"Talbot and his men," Scott told them. "They're making a raid on the village. Get your rifles and take cover. He won't be playing games like he was at the church service."

There were not enough firearms in the village for a strong defense. Some of the men, like Hunting Wolf, had produced old rifles or rusted handguns. Hunting Wolf had succeeded in getting most of the men under cover. The domed grass houses offered little protection, but the frame buildings and earthen lodges should serve for cover.

Scott retrieved his Winchester from the sorrel and shooed her away. Rifle in hand, he ran to join Brother Sam and Matt. They were in a wooden structure that appeared to serve as both home and storage shed. The door and a single window offered a view of the hill. Brother Sam and his son flanked the window. Their rifles were held ready. Matt's face was strained. The reverend's was hard. Though a man of God, Brother Sam had no qualms about taking up arms to defend innocent lives. He was fighting for the right things.

Scott dropped to one knee beside the door and lifted his Winchester. The village inhabitants, he saw with relief, had all taken cover. He waited for the riders to crest the hill. But the skyline remained empty.

Scott stiffened. "Come on!" he said sharply. "They're moving in from the rear!" He dodged out the door. He heard Brother Sam and Matt behind him. They asked no questions. He glimpsed Hunting Wolf in a doorway and waved a reassuring hand.

Talbot was no fool, Scott calculated. He knew his approach had been spotted and that the village had been given a few crucial minutes to prepare. He would not lead his men into the teeth of waiting enemies. He would, instead, send some of them around to strike at the village from the other side. Only then, when the defenders had been distracted, would he lead the remainder of his men in a direct frontal attack.

Scott knew his calculations were correct and berated himself for not perceiving the danger sooner. He hoped he was not too late.

He led the way around the storage house and past a grass hut at a run. He pulled up short. Automatically he levered his Winchester. Six riders were coming down fast upon the village from the rear. The cultivated fields had slowed them, but they were already dangerously close.

Scott sprang for the protection of an earthen lodge and pressed close to its dirt wall. He saw Sam and Matt taking cover in a lean-to connected to a house. Scott snapped the butt of the Winchester to his shoulder. There was no problem with range now. The rifle punched back hard as he fired. Out in the field a rider toppled backward from his horse.

Angry shouts and gunfire answered him. He fired again and missed. A bullet sprayed dirt from the wall above his head. Somebody was a good mounted shot.

He was aware of the twin reports of Matt's and Sam's rifles.

At the same moment he heard gunfire erupt from the far side of the village. Talbot was pushing home the rest of the attack. Scott hoped grimly that he was meeting more than he'd bargained for.

The foremost rider had cleared the cultivated ground, and reins in his teeth, a six-gun blazing in each hand, he rode like a professional fighting man as he bore down on Scott. Bullets chipped dirt over Scott's head and at his side. Coolly Scott lined up the Winchester and pulled the trigger. The gunman sloped sideways in the saddle, and then, as the reins dropped from his teeth, he slid limply from his horse. Here was one professional fighting man who had gambled his life once too often.

Three remaining attackers were cutting their losses in flight. Between them, Sam and Matt had accounted for the third gunman, who lay sprawled in the field. The firing from the front of the village had stopped.

"Keep the rear covered," Scott ordered. Matt nodded tightly. Scott slipped back to the storage house and surveyed the scene.

The still forms of two men lay a little below the crest of the hill. One of them had an arrow in his chest. No other attackers were in sight. Talbot had expected the defenders to be distracted by the rear attack when he led his remaining force over the hill. Instead he had met organized resistance and had suffered losses. Two men down was not a particularly good score, given the advantage of an ambush, but few of the Indians would be trained fighters.

Had Talbot given up the attack? Scott wondered.

"Colton?" The voice seemed to ring out of the sky.

"I'm here, Talbot," Scott called back after a moment. He fingered the lever action of his Winchester.

"I thought that was you. It almost *had* to be you to organize these mangy curs into a fighting force in a couple of minutes' time." Deep anger vibrated in Talbot's rolling tones.

"You lost, Talbot. Give it up."

"I only lose battles," came the disembodied voice, "never wars."

"You've lost this one," Scott shouted back. He scanned the skyline intently. Was Talbot employing some new diversionary tactic by keeping him talking?

"Wrong, Colton. *You've* lost. You and the preacher. I'm finished using an easy hand on you. From now on, it's a hard fist and a loaded gun."

"You'll have to do better than you did today. These Indians cut you in half. They'll be ready for you next time too."

"I won't give you any more chances. You and the preacher get out of the Territory!"

"I'm not leaving, Talbot!" Brother Sam's voice rang out. He had appeared at Scott's side. "You can't run us out."

There was a pause. "Preacher?" Talbot called at last.

"That's right, Talbot. I'm here."

"Say your prayers, preacher!" Talbot's voice rolled like thunder.

"I'll say them for you," Brother Sam shouted back.

Scott's palms ached against the wood and metal of

the Winchester. "Talbot," he called, "let's settle this. You and me. Fist and gun!"

Again a pause. "Another time, Colton. I've had my say. You remember it."

Scott glanced at Brother Sam. The preacher's face was grim. His expression said there was no more to say. Scott levered the Winchester and fired a shot into the sky.

It was as good an answer as any.

Chapter Seven

The jagged teeth of the big crosscut saw chewed through the last fibers of the heavy board. The two-foot section that had been severed fell to the ground. Scott and Matt straightened and grinned at each other across the saw they had been wielding.

"That's the last one," Matt said with relief.

Scott drew a forearm across his sweating forehead. "Let's drink some of that water," he suggested.

They sat down beneath a big cottonwood at the edge of the construction area. Scott offered the jug to Matt, who gestured at him to go first. Scott drank thirstily, then passed the jug to Matt. The afternoon wind blowing across the prairie felt good. He glanced over at Matt as the latter finished his drink. "You did good at the Indian village yesterday."

Matt was pleased at the compliment, although Scott could tell he tried to conceal it. "You and Pa did most of it," he replied. "Pa dropped one." He looked down sheepishly. "My hands were shaking too hard to hit anything."

"So were mine the first time I came under fire," Scott assured him. "You stood up to them, and you fought back. That's what counts."

Matt toyed idly with a broken twig. "Pa says it's important to know how to use a gun, since you may have to use it sometimes. But he says you need to be careful not to make using a gun the most important thing in your life."

"Your pa's a wise man," Scott said. "I wish I'd known that about guns when I was your age."

"Somebody's coming," Ruth called from the camp.

Scott pushed himself smoothly to his feet. His palm brushed the butt of his .45. Matt stood also. Brother Sam was just emerging from the church as they entered the camp.

Ruth was awaiting them. She wore a blue bandanna over her blond hair. Scott thought that she looked lovely.

"It's somebody in a buggy," she informed them. "I think maybe a woman."

Scott squinted down the road. "Belle Tanner," he said tonelessly. He felt the others look at him. He kept his eyes on the approaching covered buggy.

Painted black, the buggy matched the dark dress and elaborate ruffled hat of its driver. A diamond pendant hung like a piece of ice at her throat. She handled the reins of the beautiful black gelding with an almost arrogant competence. Lobo trotted by the vehicle's side, tongue lolling.

Scott realized that he and the Prentiss family had

drawn together in a tight grouping. Ruth was close beside him as they waited. Belle pulled the big gelding to a prancing halt before them. Lobo regarded them balefully from behind one of the front wheels.

"Hello, Belle," Scott greeted her drily. "Have you come to church?"

The look she gave him smoldered with unreadable emotions. She studied each of them in turn. Her gaze seemed to linger longest on Ruth.

Brother Sam stepped forward. "Welcome," he said. "I'm Sam Prentiss. May we help you?"

Her gaze shifted to him. The preacher and the saloon owner gauged each other.

"So you're the reverend," Belle said, returning the greeting at last.

"Yes. These are my children, Ruth and Matt."

Belle ignored the introductions. "You're a stubborn man, Reverend."

"Sometimes a man has to be stubborn to accomplish anything worthwhile," Sam answered smoothly. "Won't you step down?"

"No, thank you." Belle broke off the conversation to look about her. She appeared to be surveying the camp and the church building. "You've done a lot of work here," she commented finally.

"We hope to do more."

Belle studied him for a moment. "I'm Belle Tanner," she said, making a belated introduction. "I own the Dark Lady Saloon as well as a number of other businesses and enterprises in Meridian."

"I know of you."

Belle's full lips moved scornfully. "And you probably don't approve of what you know."

Brother Sam shrugged. "You're as welcome in my church as anyone."

Belle looked around the camp again. "I hear you had a nice meeting Sunday morning, until it got broken up."

"It didn't get broken up," Brother Sam corrected her. "We went ahead with the service and dinner even after the disturbance."

Belle shook her head as if frustrated with a small child. She tapped a crimson-painted fingernail against the metal frame of the buggy's cover. Watching her, Scott wondered what motive she had in coming here. Her gaze swung to him. "I see you're still working for him." Her voice was almost challenging.

"I haven't had any better offers."

Her lips thinned. The gelding tossed its head impatiently. Lobo was as motionless as a stone idol.

"Let me be frank, Reverend," she addressed Brother Sam again.

"Please."

"I don't care personally whether you start a church here or not. As far as I'm concerned, you're welcome to do so, for all the good it will do you. But I own a big piece of this town, and it wasn't easy to come by. Meridian is important to me, and what goes on in Meridian is important to me also."

"It's important to me too," Brother Sam said.

Belle drew a deep breath. "You and your church have caused quite a stir in town, Reverend."

Brother Sam grinned slightly. "I know."

"Brawls in the street"—her eyes flicked to Scott—"a

near riot on Sunday morning. I hear there have even been some killings out at that sorry Indian town."

"We didn't look for any of this trouble." Despite his words, Brother Sam's tone was neither meek nor defensive.

"It doesn't matter whether you looked for it or not. It's here." Belle's voice had grown sharper. "Your presence is disrupting this town, and I don't like it."

"The men that were killed were outlaws. They were attacking the Indians without provocation. I regret their deaths almost certainly more than you do. But I fail to see any bad effect it can have on Meridian."

"Where there have been killings, there will be more. Outlaws or not, it doesn't matter. Killings are bad for a town. They make it look bad to outsiders. They spoil its reputation. We depend on Guthrie for much of our business and trade. If Meridian gets a name for bloodshed and violence, the citizens of Guthrie will shun us. It could mean real harm to our economy."

"The nature of your town's commerce spawns violence and bloodshed, Miss Tanner," Brother Sam said. "Don't blame my church. If you want to rid Meridian of violence, then cleanse it of the vice in which you trade."

Belle's nostrils flared. Scott looked at Lobo. The wolf dog was bristling silently.

"I didn't come here to argue." Belle's voice was tight. "Like I told you, the success or failure of your church doesn't matter to me. But I don't want to see any more trouble caused hereabouts because of it. I'll make you an offer, Reverend. It's this: I'll buy your land and your church from you. Then you take the money and leave the Territory. Go somewhere else to start your church, somewhere where the town wants a church, and where it will be easier on you and your family. I'll pay you ten thousand dollars cash for your land, right now."

Scott caught his breath. He heard Ruth gasp beside him. It was an extravagant amount. Belle was being more than generous in her offer.

Brother Sam shook his head. "The land isn't for sale," he said firmly.

A slow flush spread over Belle's exquisite features. "Think about it," she urged. "Ten thousand dollars. Think what you could do with that kind of money in starting a church somewhere else."

"I don't need to go somewhere else to start a church," Brother Sam told her calmly. "I've started one here. This is where I belong."

Belle sucked in her breath in exasperation. "I'll give you some time to consider it."

The thought came to Scott that Belle was trying to buy Sam Prentiss just as she had tried to buy him. But Brother Sam did not appear to be even tempted. "I don't need to consider it. The answer is no. And the offer to visit our services is still open."

"You've made some dangerous enemies in this region, Reverend. I really think you should reconsider."

"I can't and won't let a man like Land Talbot dictate where I have my ministry. I answer to a higher authority than that man."

"Land Talbot may just end your ministry," Belle said emphatically.

"He can try."

Belle shook her head. She looked to Scott. "Can you talk any sense into him?"

"He's making sense so far as I've heard," Scott said. He was intensely aware of Ruth standing close at his side.

Belle shifted her attention to Matt and Ruth. She seemed about to address them, then appeared to think better of it. "I've done all I can," she said to Brother Sam. "Now you'll have to suffer the consequences of your choice, Reverend."

"So will we all," Brother Sam answered her quietly.

The toss of her head was every bit as spirited and impatient as that of the fine black gelding. She snapped the reins, then laid them hard against the horse's neck. Scott and the others stepped back as the animal pulled the buggy around in a sharp turn. Lobo danced beside the wheels. Abruptly Belle yanked the gelding once more to a halt.

Her eyes flashed fire like the diamond at her throat. She looked at Scott, then turned her head and deliberately studied Ruth. Ruth trembled, but she stood firm and met the older woman's gaze defiantly.

Belle said from between her even white teeth, "You've made your choice too, Mr. Colton?"

Scott nodded slightly.

Belle's head lifted in perverse triumph. "I can see why you made your choice," she said with meaning. "I told you she wasn't a child."

Ruth gasped in startled outrage. "Good-bye, Belle," Scott said.

Belle snapped the reins angrily. She drove the buggy

recklessly back down the road toward town. Lobo loped in silent menace alongside.

"How dare she have that much nerve!" Ruth burst out. She turned to Scott. "She looked at you like—like she owned you."

"She's used to owning men, I'd say." Brother Sam swung about from staring after Belle's departure. "In fact, she's probably used to owning anything she wants. A dangerous woman. I'm sorry I angered her, but she needed to hear the truth."

"Did you see that dog?" Matt breathed in awe. "He looked ready to go for us at any minute, especially you, Scott."

"They say he's a man killer," Scott told him. "He's probably more dangerous than any gunman you'll ever run up against."

"I knew there was a need for a church here," Brother Sam murmured almost to himself. "I just didn't realize how great a need." Then he addressed the others resolutely: "Let's go back to work."

Scott followed Matt back toward the lumber. The boards they had cut still needed to be stacked. Ruth slipped in front of him. "I'm glad you turned her down," she whispered.

"I'd do it again," Scott told her.

She blushed prettily and smiled a soft smile. She turned back toward the tent. Scott went to help Matt with the boards, and they had just stacked them when Ruth once again sought them out. "Some more people are coming from town," she reported.

This seemed to be their day for visitors, Scott thought. He checked the .45 again. But the party that rode into camp did not appear to offer any immediate threat of violence. Four of them were in a double-seated carriage. The remaining two rode fine, blooded horses. They had a well-dressed, well-fed, sleek, and prosperous look to them. Merchants and businessmen, Scott pegged them. Town fathers.

Brother Sam greeted them warmly and then introduced Scott and his children. The newcomers identified themselves in turn. One of them owned a hotel, another a freight office. The third was a real estate broker. Of the remaining three, one owned a café and another had a barber shop. The sixth man introduced himself as Conrad Snideley, the mayor of Meridian.

"I'm honored, Mayor," Brother Sam told him.

"Of course, the post of mayor is mostly an honorary one," Snidely said with obviously false humility. "I'm also a store owner. But, as mayor, I do, in a sense, speak for the town fathers and the good townspeople on many matters." He was a short, round man with a fringe of silver hair and a puffy face. His hands were heavy with diamond and gold rings. "I thought perhaps it was time for us to pay you a visit, padre." The title seemed to echo faintly with mockery.

Scott caught Ruth's quick and significant exchange of glances with her brother. Obviously they disliked and mistrusted the town's self-proclaimed spokesman. And so did Scott.

"Of course, of course." If Brother Sam detected any mockery, it did not show in his courteous manner. "Scott and Matt, would you get us a couple of the new pews so we can be more comfortable out here?"

By the time Scott and Matt had complied, Snidely

was well into a lecture on the remarkable prosperity enjoyed by Meridian in its short history. "Our luck has been golden," he continued. "Oh, thank you, boys." As he settled himself into the rough-hewn pew, Scott thought of a toad squatting down to wait for an unwary june bug.

Some of Snideley's companions joined him on the pew. A couple remained standing uneasily. All of them seemed content to let Snidely continue as their spokesman. Scott studied their faces and knew his earlier evaluation had been correct. These were not men of violence, but they were men of power and influence within their own limited spheres. Money and what it could buy were their weapons.

Brother Sam seated himself on the second pew facing them. He leaned earnestly forward, forearms on his knees. Matt and Ruth sat on either side of him. Scott stayed on his feet.

"Between us here, we represent a good part of Meridian's respectable businesses that are not owned or controlled by, uh, another single party," Snidely stated pompously. "And I believe I can safely say that we speak for, or have the backing of, virtually all such interests in Meridian."

Scott interpreted that to mean the business owners who weren't under Belle Tanner's crimson-nailed thumb. But how much influence did she wield over them just the same? he wondered.

"We, that is, the other businessmen and I, decided that it was time we visited with you, padre, about the future of your little church here in Meridian."

"I welcome this opportunity," Brother Sam assured him. "I appreciate your coming here."

Snidely made some noncommittal snorting noises. "Well, padre, as you can understand, our interests and our futures pretty much depend on the continued prosperity of Meridian."

"Of course."

"That economy, as you probably well know, is based on a wide variety of town citizens and fringe inhabitants of the surrounding areas. We don't like to see one group disadvantaged or inconvenienced by other interests. It disturbs the status quo, if you know what I mean."

"I'm not sure I do, Mr. Mayor," Brother Sam said quietly.

Snidely shifted uncomfortably. None of his companions seemed inclined to assist him. "Let me put it this way, padre. We have a good balance of interests right now in Meridian, everything considered. All of us find our businesses to be profitable. We would regret it if anything disturbed that."

"Are you implying that the presence of this church might upset the balance?" Brother Sam asked, his voice still quiet.

"Well, yes, it's a possibility, of course." Snidely seized the opening with apparent relief. "You can surely understand that."

"I can?"

Snidely became flustered. He clenched his fleshy, ringed hands. "When a church comes to a community, it can change things."

"That, I hope, is the point of having a church, Mr. Snidely."

"Yes, well, but some communities are better suited to churches than others. Don't you agree?"

"I think every community should have a church, Mr. Mayor."

"Maybe not this one," a new voice said. "At least not just yet." He was one of the men who had remained standing. He was tall and silver haired. "I'm Ward Salyer, Reverend. I deal in real estate in this area. I think what Conrad is trying to say is that a large portion of the Meridian community has no need or desire for a church. That segment of the community constitutes a good part of our livelihood. This being the case, I don't think any of us here, or our families, can offer any encouragement in your efforts to start a church. And it might be tough going without our support—you know, with donations and attendance, and such." Salyer paused and at last had the grace to look slightly embarrassed. "We thought you'd like to know all this in order to evaluate your church's future here."

Murmurs of assent came from the others.

Brother Sam rose slowly to his feet as if he were taking the pulpit before a crowd of sinners. He regarded the visitors sternly. "As I recall, gentlemen, none of you were at the service Sunday morning, nor do I remember seeing you or any of your family members at any of the other services we've held so far." The businessmen shifted uncomfortably beneath his gaze. "From your words, I'm guessing also that you haven't told anyone else of the church or suggested they attend, nor have you yet made any financial contribution to our work here."

Only Salyer continued to look at Brother Sam. Snidely's face was strained, and, like the others, he stared at the ground.

Brother Sam nodded in confirmation. "Since, by your own admission, none of you has attended or ever plans to do so, why should it possibly concern me whether or not you support this church in any fashion whatsoever?" When no one had a reply, he continued in a milder voice, "But from the response we've seen so far, gentlemen, there is a large segment of the people who do want a church very much, and it is to them that I will continue to minister and to them that I would have to answer if I gave in to your pressure to leave."

Salyer finally spoke: "One day soon, Reverend, you may be sorry for taking that kind of attitude."

"And one day, in another life, you may be sorry for your own attitudes."

"I'll stick to worrying about this life for now," Salyer said.

"That's your choice. My choice is to build this church. And I'd welcome you and your families in attendance if you ever change your minds."

The businessmen were red faced to a man. Their postures were stiff. Salyer made a sharp, angry gesture. He turned wordlessly and strode to his horse. The others followed him.

Scott looked at Brother Sam. The pastor's face was still stern, but sorrow was there as well, and he drew a deep breath as the carriage rolled away.

"That's not fair!" Matt exclaimed after a moment. "We haven't done anything to them! What business do they have treating us like that?"

Brother Sam waved a tired hand. "Forget it, son.

You'll run into those types no matter where you go or what you do with your life. You can't change their minds. That's something they have to do themselves."

"Once the church is open, they'll start coming," Ruth predicted with her customary optimism.

"You may be right," her father acknowledged. "I've seen stranger things happen. They were right about one point, though. Having a church in town can change people as well as circumstances."

Scott studied Brother Sam for any sign of despair or defeat. In short order he had been served notice that the most powerful elements in Meridian's political and economic structure had no desire to have the church completed. This had come on top of physical violence directed against him and his family.

Brother Sam appeared to have little concern for such opposition. He grinned at Scott and his children. "I'll give you three a day off tomorrow," he told them. "I'd like you to take the wagon and make a swing out through the countryside, inviting the farmers and their families to church on Sunday."

Ruth turned a happy smile to Scott. Her eyes were dancing. "That'll be fun!" she said to her father.

"I don't like it," Scott said. "It's dangerous for you to be here alone, Sam."

Brother Sam dismissed his concern with a casual wave of his hand. "I'll be all right."

Scott frowned. "Maybe you and Matt should go," he suggested.

Brother Sam shook his head. "No, I think it's better my way. People expect the preacher to ask them to church. But an invitation from Ruth and Matt would mean more to them. And you need to be along to make sure Talbot and his boys don't take a hand to interfere."

"What if they interfere here?" Scott asked.

"Scott, we can't let Talbot control our lives. I'll take reasonable precautions, such as sending you along with Ruth and Matt, but I won't let Land Talbot dictate how we live or how I conduct my ministry. Understand?"

Scott understood that this whole idea of Brother Sam's was probably a mistake. He did not want to let the issue rest. His instincts rebelled against the arrangement. But he had no authority to tell Brother Sam what to do, particularly when it came to running the church.

"All right," he said. "I'll go along with them, but you keep your back to a wall while we're gone."

"I'll be careful," Brother Sam promised. "Matt, give me a hand with these pews."

Ruth came close to Scott when her father and brother were out of earshot. Her touch on his arm was light. "Father's right," she told him. "It really will be good for Matt and me to get out and meet the people and invite them to the services. You'll see."

Scott was sure that his misgivings showed on his face. "I hope so," he said.

They set out in the cool of the morning. Scott was on his sorrel mare. Matt and Ruth shared the seat of the wagon. Matt handled the reins with a sure grip.

Scott glanced back once. Brother Sam waved a final time, then turned toward the church. He had been working on finishing the pews inside. Scott quelled the unease that still coiled in him. Brother Sam had added a final comment the night before: "Talbot may have given up after the losses he suffered at the Indian village." But Scott didn't think so.

"Don't look so grim," Ruth chided him now. She was bright and cheerful and pretty in a yellow dress.

Scott managed a grin back at her. It wasn't hard. He didn't want to let his cynicism spoil the outing. Maybe Brother Sam was right, and their problems were over.

Matt eyed his sister and Scott, and whispered something to Ruth. She blushed, giggled, elbowed him, and refused to look at Scott for a few moments. Matt appeared pleased with himself. Scott found his concerns fading in the face of their good spirits.

They stopped at a farmer's home a few miles out from the church. The house was built of sod blocks cut from the hard ground. Eventually they would decompose in the elements, but in the meantime they made cheap and practical material. The mound of a storm cellar was nearby. Scott guessed that the farmer and his family had staked the land during the run. The cellar had been dug immediately and had provided living quarters until the sod house could be built. A frame house would be constructed one day. It was a common pattern among the tough breed of homesteaders who had occupied the Territory when it opened for settlement.

The farmer's wife emerged from the house to greet them. She carried a child in one arm, and two older children lurked in the doorway of the house. The woman's weathered face lit up warmly at Ruth's introduction.

"Of course, you're the preacher's daughter, the one who sings so pretty. I'm Janey Brown. Danny," she told the oldest of the children, "go get your pa and big brother from the field. We got company. The preacher's kids are here."

Scott could see the two distant figures in the cultivated land that had been carved from the prairie. One of them worked the plow behind a draft horse. The other walked ahead, bending frequently to remove rocks from in front of the plow.

By the time the man and his son came tramping in from the field, his wife had Scott and his companions seated at a handmade table in the shade of the sod house. She and Ruth were visiting like old friends. Matt was making overtures of friendship to the other child, who still lurked near the door to the house. Scott felt a kind of awkward peace with the situation.

He recognized the farmer from the Sunday-morning service. The man greeted them gruffly but with an underlying warmth. His hand was as hard and weathered as the land he worked. He introduced himself as Seth Brown and let his wife carry most of the talk.

"We were so glad when your father started his church here," she was saying to Ruth. "I'd been wanting one for us and the children. Seth promised me we'd make it a point to go every Sunday." Her husband nodded agreement. "It was just awful what those men did, riding through the service like that," Janey hurried on. She seemed eager to talk. Scott guessed that the family's social contacts were sparse.

Seth eyed Scott. His gaze lingered on Scott's .45. The farmer himself had carried a battered old carbine in with him from the field. "You kin to the pastor?" he asked.

Scott shook his head. "Just helping him out." He was more than ever aware of the gap separating him from these honest, God-fearing people.

Seth nodded as if Scott's answer was sufficient. "The preacher seems a good man."

"We really must be going," Ruth said, rising from the table. "But I'll see you this Sunday, Janey."

They pulled out amidst promises from the women to see each other again, and even a taciturn farewell from Seth.

"They're good people," Ruth said once they were away. She had clearly enjoyed her visit with Janey.

Scott contrasted the solid integrity of the young farm couple with the shallow hypocrisy of the representatives of Meridian's business community who had visited the camp the day before. He could begin to understand Brother Sam's determined dedication and Ruth's sincere optimism. The church did fulfill a need in the community and whole area.

That belief was reinforced throughout the day. On a wide swing around Meridian, they dropped in on many farming and ranching families, some of whom Scott had seen at the service. Like the Browns, they were eager to visit with the pastor's family. Others they called on were strangers, but even these, for the most part, greeted them hospitably.

Ruth's enthusiasm remained undimmed, and Matt, too, seemed to be enjoying himself, particularly at one homestead where there was a pretty teenaged girl. He spent most of that stop talking with her out near the wagon. Later, it was Ruth's turn to make a mischievous comment to him about sparking. She and Scott both laughed at the embarrassed expression on his face.

With the afternoon waning, Matt headed the team back toward Meridian. A friendly spotted dog from their last stop trotted alongside the wagon for a distance before turning back homeward.

Scott was tired, but it was a satisfying tiredness. He had said and done little enough through most of the visits, but he had the good feeling of having been a part of a worthwhile endeavor. He was surprised to realize that he did not want the day to end. Brother Sam and his church certainly seemed to be working a change in him, he reflected.

"You look happy," Ruth told him with a smile.

Scott grinned in acknowledgment. He looked ahead and saw the tendril of smoke growing from the horizon.

The hot prairie wind turned cold.

"I'm going to ride on ahead," he said.

He thought he had kept his tone even, but Ruth's gaze sharpened. "What's wrong?" she demanded.

Scott could not keep his eyes from the smoke. It was thickening now to a grayish column. Ruth followed the direction of his gaze.

"Oh, no!" she whispered.

Faint popping sounds jabbed at Scott's eardrums.

"Gunfire!" Matt cried. "That smoke's coming from the church!" He let out a yell and urged the team forward.

Scott didn't wait. He drummed his heels hard against the sorrel's sides and put her into a run.

The wagon fell behind him. He could hear Matt's urgent yells to goad the team to greater speed. The hooves of the sorrel hammered at the hard soil. The dry wind of his passage rushed past Scott's face. Ahead of him the column of smoke thickened and grew. He could already smell its harsh scent. Tears from the wind blurred his vision.

Off to his left he saw a pack of mounted men riding hard toward the open plains. They might have been within rifle shot, but he didn't slow. His breath raced in his lungs as if it were he and not the sorrel who ran.

He tore into the trees bordering the creek. Where once he had glimpsed a steeple through their branches, he saw the tops of leaping orange flames. He burst into the clearing. An enormous bonfire roared toward the sky where the church had once stood. The heat blasted at Scott's face. He was barely aware of it. Brother Sam Prentiss sprawled motionless at the fire's edge.

Chapter Eight

R uth jumped to her feet as the doctor emerged from his surgery. Scott and Matt joined her. It had been a long wait.

Lewis Perdue was Meridian's only doctor. He was tall and spare, and his lined face was stern. "The reverend should recover, given time," he announced without preamble.

"Praise the Lord," Ruth said thankfully.

"He was shot in the chest. The ribs slowed the bullet. I removed it and repaired what damage I could. His recovery depends on the care he receives."

"I'll take care of him," Ruth asserted.

Perdue nodded. "He's a strong man. I've used opium to keep him asleep for now. He should begin to come out of it by late tomorrow morning. If he seems in satisfactory condition then, you'll have to take him with you. I have no room for long-term patients here at my clinic." He looked away from them as he spoke.

Scott wondered with a tinge of bitterness if the physician's attitude would be different if the patient wasn't the pastor of the church that was apparently so unpopular in Meridian. It was probably not a fair thought. Perdue had been willing enough to handle the emergency when they brought Brother Sam to him hours ago. Acting with professional alacrity, Perdue had assisted them in getting Brother Sam's unwieldy form into his surgery. The wait had been a fretful and tiring one. Ruth and Matt had prayed while they clutched hands. They had included Scott in their circle. He had bowed his head and added his own awkward and silent prayer.

"I'll check on him daily until he's better," Perdue promised. "Where will you have him?"

"Out at our camp," Scott answered immediately. "Where the church was." He felt both Ruth and Matt look at him sharply.

"Good enough. Now I'll have to ask you to leave. It's late and I need to be closing."

"But—" Ruth began a protest.

"My living quarters are here," Perdue cut her off smoothly. "I'll check on your father through the night. You come back here late tomorrow morning."

Ruth wanted to object further, but Perdue's unyielding demeanor appeared to baffle her. She acquiesced with a small shrug of frustration.

"Your father's a lucky man, Miss Prentiss," Perdue added.

"Luck had nothing to do with it," she told him firmly.

Perdue did not argue. "I'll see you all tomorrow." He gazed unblinkingly at them for a moment. "Be careful. I handle lots of gunshot wounds among the rowdies and transients and rabble here. I've come to expect that. I don't like having good people shot, however."

He turned sharply away, leaving them to their own interpretations of his statement.

"Doctor?" Ruth said quickly.

Perdue looked back over his shoulder with a raised eyebrow.

"Can we see him, just for a moment?"

"I told you, he's asleep and will remain so for some hours."

"Please," Ruth implored.

Even Perdue could not resist that. "Very well," he relented. "But only for one minute. Precisely that."

He led the way back into the interior of his clinic. Ruth clung to Scott's arm. Her fingers dug tightly into his muscles. Matt's face was pale.

Brother Sam lay rigid on a bed, his torso encircled by bandages and his face blistered. He looked gaunt and shrunken. His breathing was labored. Ruth's grip on Scott's arm tightened. Matt stepped forward hesitantly.

At least the man was alive, Scott thought gratefully. Maybe their prayers *had* been answered. When he had flung himself from the sorrel to kneel by Brother Sam's prone body in the blast-furnace heat of the leaping flames, he had not thought the pastor was alive. Frantically he had dragged Brother Sam clear of the heat. His fumbling fingers detected a fluttering pulse. Momentarily he had expected it to cease. Then, miraculously, Brother Sam had opened his eyes and managed in a faltering whisper, "Should've listened to you." Scott stripped off his shirt and pressed it against the wound. "It was Talbot." Sam's voice was faint. "I tried to stay in the church and fight them off. They set it on fire. I had to come out then. They shot me."

Scott tried to tell him not to speak further, but could not find words. Then it had not mattered, because Brother Sam lapsed back into unconsciousness.

They had loaded him gently into the bed of the wagon. Ruth held his head in her lap as Scott drove the wagon. Blood from her father's wound had stained her yellow dress.

"He'll get well. I know he will," Ruth spoke at last as they hovered over the still form on the bed.

"That's long enough," Perdue said with gentle firmness that brooked no argument. He ushered them out of the room.

Outside on the street it was dark. Gas lamps provided wavering illumination. The clinic was in Meridian's more prosperous business section. Down the street, the clamor of the Friday-night revelry issued from the garish saloons. Scott could see the elaborate facade of the Dark Lady, where he guessed that Belle Tanner was doing a good night's business.

For a moment the three of them stood on the boardwalk. Scott hugged Ruth to him with an arm around her shoulders. He felt her sag against him. Matt stood on his other side. It seemed only natural to put a brotherly arm around the youth's shoulders as well.

"Let's go home," Scott said.

They rode in silence. Ruth sat beside Scott. She buried her face in her hands. Scott realized that she was crying in silent grief. Matt was a tense, brooding shadow in the wagon's bed.

"I'm so glad he's alive." Ruth lifted a tear-streaked

face. "But it was such an awful thing to see him hurt like that."

They left Meridian behind. The night was black and solid around them. Scott brushed his hand against the butt of the .45. He remembered vaguely a visit by Zeke Cantrell during their long wait at the clinic. The stable owner had reported that a pump wagon manned by Meridian's volunteer fire department had prevented the blaze from spreading. Scott wondered if their slowness in responding to the fire had been deliberate.

He brushed the butt of the .45 again, then forced his hand away from it. "A hard fist and a loaded gun," Talbot had warned at the Indian village. He had been as good as his word. Brother Sam had been left for dead. Scott wondered who had pulled the trigger. The pale face of Strike Foster seemed to hover in the darkness. It would be like Talbot to let his pet gunfighter do his dirty work.

"I'll take care of Father until he's well," Ruth vowed again. She seemed to summon strength from expressing her plans. "The doctor said he'd come out every day, and I know I can learn how to change the bandages and keep the wound clean. I've tended wounds before, at least smaller ones. I can fix broth for him to eat until he's stronger."

Her optimism drew Scott from his brooding reverie. "You're the best nurse he could have," he told her. "And the one he'd pick if he had a choice."

He pulled the team to a halt in the ruins of their camp. The church was a black pile of rubble in the gloom. A single ember glowed from its depths like the eye of some demonic watcher. The smell of smoke was still strong.

Scott climbed stiffly down from the wagon, and then he turned to lift Ruth out. "Let's see if we can find a lantern and figure out where we can sleep," he suggested. "We'll take stock tomorrow."

Matt jumped from the wagon in a single angry movement. He prowled in the direction of the charred pile of rubble.

"The tent's down, but it doesn't seem to be ripped," Ruth reported. She was groping over the canvas material.

Scott found an intact lantern and lit it. Its glow cast a wan illumination across the scene.

Matt stood by the edge of the rubble. He kicked at a charred board in a sudden violent fury. "I don't know why we even came back!" he exclaimed. "There's nothing here!"

"The church is here," Scott said quietly.

Matt gestured sharply at the ruins. "There's the church!"

Scott kept his tone even: "You told me the first day we met that you don't need a building to have a church." He was conscious that Ruth had drawn close to his side.

"That was different!" Matt objected. "They've burned us out, almost killed Pa. And we weren't hurting them! What are we doing here, anyway?"

"Building a church."

Matt rounded on him angrily. "Are we going to just stand here and let them get away with it?" he demanded. "Why aren't we going after them?"

Scott restrained his hand from moving instinctively to grip the .45. A part of him responded on a dark, barbaric level to Matt's demand. "I don't think your pa would want us to handle it that way," he heard himself say.

"He's always said you might have to fight sometimes!"

"That's just it." Scott's voice sounded mild in his own ears. "We don't have to fight now. Do you see anyone attacking us?"

"They'll be back! You know they'll be back!"

"Then we'll defend ourselves when they come."

"How can just the three of us fight them?"

"You leave that to me. It's my specialty." Scott injected more assurance into his voice than he actually felt.

Matt stared at him. The youth's face was an angry mask in the pale light.

"Scott's right, Matt," Ruth said. "Father would want us to do just what we're doing." Her voice was soothing and patient. "Help me with the tent."

Gradually Matt relaxed. Scott realized that, with his grief and anger, the youth was close to tears. Scott turned away, saying, "I'll tend to the horses."

With Ruth diplomatically letting Matt take charge, the tent was erected by the time Scott finished. "Oh, it's such a mess," Ruth said, pressing her hands to her face as she surveyed their jumbled belongings. "I want to start cleaning it up right now."

"Go on to bed," Scott advised. "This can all wait."

She nodded. "You're right. I just want to be doing something."

"I know." Scott thought of his own dark yearnings for vengeance. Sometimes, as he had just told her, it was best to wait before taking action.

Matt had retired with a blanket to the far side of the camp, Scott saw. Ruth touched his arm gently. He looked down at her.

"Thank you for being so strong," she said softly. "I don't know if Matt and I could've handled this if you hadn't been here."

Scott thought of her courageous optimism in the face of all odds. He recalled Matt's untested strength. "You would've both done just fine," he assured her.

She shook her head. "No. You said just the right things to Matt. Father will be proud."

"On one level I agree with Matt," Scott admitted.

"I know. That's why it means so much to me that you've said and done what you have tonight."

"Two weeks ago I couldn't have done it. All of you have been good for me. Especially you."

They clung together. Their kiss was born of love as much as passion.

"Pray that Father will get well," she murmured against his chest.

"I will," Scott promised.

Later, lying on his blanket, Scott imagined her moving gracefully about inside the tent as she prepared for bed. Exhaustion had settled over him, pulling at his eyelids and numbing his mind. Before he slept, he remembered his promise. His prayer was for the healing of Brother Sam. But it was also one of gratitude for the presence of Ruth Prentiss in his life.

When he awoke in the cool light of dawning, he saw

Matt standing near the charred remnants of the church. Matt glanced around at him as he approached.

"Get any sleep?" Scott asked.

"A little."

Scott looked in the direction of his gaze. The wooden cross that had surmounted the church had somehow survived the fire. It must have toppled clear as the structure beneath it was consumed. It lay untouched near the edge of the rubble.

"What do we do now?" Matt asked sullenly. He still stared at the cross.

The words came easily to Scott: "We start over."

Matt looked around at him with a flicker of last night's anger. "Start over with what? There's nothing here."

"How long have you and your pa and Ruth been working on the church?" Scott asked him. "A month or so?"

"I guess."

"There was nothing here before you all came," Scott reminded him. "If we start now, we can have things back to the way they were by the time your father recovers."

"And we just let Talbot and his crew get away with it? We just wait for them to come back and do it again?"

"I told you, that's my worry."

Obviously the answer didn't satisfy Matt. But he didn't argue. Scott left him there and headed down toward the creek to clean up. After a moment he heard Matt's footsteps behind him.

When they returned, Ruth was trying to salvage some supplies from the mess for breakfast. She waved and called a greeting to them. Seen by daylight, the camp was a shambles, but it could have been worse, Scott reflected. Their belongings and supplies were still basically intact. And, he reminded himself, Brother Sam was still alive.

"Company coming," Ruth called.

A battered old prairie schooner, without its canvas top, came creaking into the camp. Seth Brown, the farmer they had visited yesterday, sat on the seat with Janey, his wife. Their children clambered about in and on the uncovered bed. Seth pulled the plodding plow horses to a halt.

Ruth hurried to greet them. Scott followed more slowly. Janey descended and hugged Ruth tightly. The two women moved away. Seth sat and surveyed the damage.

"How's the preacher?" he asked Scott.

"Hit bad. But the doc says he'll pull through."

Seth gave his understanding nod. He climbed down to the ground. His look swept the camp again. "Talbot?"

"Yeah."

"We heard what happened. Would've come sooner if we'd known. I saw the smoke, but didn't know it was the church. I'm sorry for you."

"Thanks," Scott said. For some reason, this taciturn farmer's concern was important to him.

Seth's children had scattered throughout the camp. Matt remained on the outskirts, observing them. The oldest boy, still Matt's junior by a few years, went over and began talking to him.

"You got any plans now?" Seth asked Scott.

"Rebuild the church."

"What if Talbot and his boys try something like this again?"

"We'll stop them."

Seth appraised him with shrewd eyes. Then he grunted and gave his nod.

"We're supposed to go into town and get Brother Sam later this morning," Scott told him.

Seth appeared to be considering something of import. "Me and Janey talked," he said finally. "We don't like what happened here, don't like outlaws such as Land Talbot running roughshod over decent God-fearing folks, especially when it's a pastor. Other farming people around here don't like it, either. They aren't happy about the preacher getting shot. I got my old carbine. The menfolk of the other families have got their guns too. If it comes to needing a guard for the pastor while he mends, or needing some protection while you get the church put up again, you just say the word. We'll be here. You can have my marker on it."

"Thanks, I appreciate the offer. Brother Sam will too." Scott tried to let Seth see the genuineness of the emotions behind his reply. "I hope it won't come to that."

"Me and the oldest boy will help some with rebuilding the church." Seth nodded toward his son, who was still visiting with Matt. "He's a good worker. Time permitting, we'll be over here some during the next few days. I reckon other folks will want to help out the same way."

"Thank you." Scott knew his answer was inadequate, but he didn't have a better one.

Seth shifted his weight as if he were uncomfortable beneath Scott's gaze. "Janey!" he called to his wife. "We need to be heading back. That field's waiting to be plowed."

Janey and Ruth returned to the wagon. They were still in intimate conversation. The older woman had her arm comfortingly around Ruth's shoulders.

"Janey fixed us some food," Ruth told Scott as they drew near. She helped Janey take two covered pots from the wagon. "We'll get these pots right back to you," Ruth promised her.

"There's no hurry." Janey began calling the children to the wagon. They responded with varying degrees of enthusiasm. Matt walked over with Seth's oldest boy.

"Oh!" Janey said, as if a thought had just struck her. "Tomorrow's Sunday. What about the church service?"

"We'll have a hymn service," Ruth told her. "A lot of singing and such." She looked anxiously at Scott. "Is that all right?"

Scott wondered what he had to do with it. He had barely even thought of tomorrow's service. Obviously, Ruth had already made plans. "Sure," he told her. "That sounds good."

She flashed him a quick smile of gratitude. "You tell everyone to come just like last week," she said to Janey.

Matt stood with them as the wagon pulled out. Seth didn't look back. He was probably already intent on his plowing. But Janey twisted around on the seat beside him to wave at them all.

"Wasn't that nice of them?" Ruth said. "She brought

us fried chicken and all the fixings. There's enough for lunch and dinner."

"I guess we can start getting some of this mess cleaned up before we go in to pick up Pa," Matt said. His earlier hostility had slipped away.

Scott drew a deep breath. "I guess so."

They made some progress before stopping to eat the breakfast Ruth prepared. Shortly after midmorning, Scott hitched up the wagon. Matt and Ruth quit their activities and watched him. Scott sensed in them a nervousness like his own. He kept recalling the pale, wasted face of Brother Sam. Had his condition worsened during the night?

He urged the horses to a faster gait than was necessary as they headed for town. Ruth was first out of the wagon when Scott pulled to a halt in front of the clinic. She did not wait on Scott's assistance to alight.

Dr. Perdue met them in the reception room. "He's doing fine," he told them. "He's coming around and should be able to go with you shortly."

Scott gave a sigh of relief.

"Can we see him?" Ruth asked.

Perdue nodded, then led the way. Even the few short hours of night and morning had made a marked difference in Brother Sam. He appeared heartier and not so frail. He was not yet conscious, although his eyelids flickered as they watched.

"I'm glad we'll be here when he awakens," Ruth said.

"Miss Prentiss, I'll need to show you how to tend to his wound," Perdue said.

"Of course. Matt, you need to know how too."

Scott stepped back and eased out the door. None of the other three seemed to notice his exit. Through the closed door, he could hear Perdue giving instructions. He left the clinic and headed down the street.

Seth Brown's offer of defensive assistance had got him to thinking. He couldn't ask farmers to go up against professional gunmen, but there was another possible source of assistance that he intended to try.

The gaudy interior of the Dark Lady was sparsely populated at this hour. Two bartenders manned the long bar. Neither of them was Johnny. Scott chose one. The fellow eyed him with a hostile curiosity as he approached.

"Tell Miss Belle that I'd like to see her," Scott told him.

The bartender wasn't happy about it, but he went. He didn't ask Scott's name. Apparently he already knew it.

"She'll see you," he reported when he returned.

Scott nodded and crossed to the massive door beneath the staircase. He didn't like being here for this purpose, but he had no other choice. Zeke Cantrell had told him on his first day that the law in Guthrie couldn't be counted on to handle problems in Meridian.

He knocked and waited. Her muffled voice bade him enter. She was posed by the bar, a full shot glass in her hand. She wore a gauzy black nightgown beneath a matching robe that was open in front. Scott tried not to look at what was revealed. As he watched, she emptied her glass with a practiced flick of her wrist and poured another in a continuation of the same motion. Lobo sat like a menacing sphinx at her feet.

"You don't drink, do you?" she said by way of greeting.

Scott shrugged. "Not usually." He felt awkward.

She shrugged and drained the shot glass again. Scott wondered how long she had been drinking that morning. Her face seemed curiously slack, as if her beauty might melt from her like wax from a candle.

"What do you want?" she asked. She poured again.

"Your help," Scott told her.

She hesitated before setting the bottle back on the bar. She held her glass but didn't drink. "What kind of help?"

"I guess you heard what happened to the pastor."

"He got shot." She snapped the glass to her lips and drained it. She poured again without looking at Scott. "He should've taken my offer."

"He says Land Talbot did it."

"So? I warned you. He's lucky to be alive."

"There was something more than luck involved."

She frowned at his remark.

"There's another way you can help," Scott told her.

What might have been suspicion stirred in her dark eyes. "How is that?"

"We plan to rebuild the church."

"You're a fool!"

"Hear me out."

She shrugged and looked away with indifference.

"If you're as interested as you say you are in stopping any more violence or bloodshed, then you should be willing to do what you can to prevent it."

"Go on." Lobo used his forelegs to push himself up to a sitting position beside his mistress. She rested a hand casually on his head. Her fingers ruffled the silver-gray fur. The wolf dog's yellow eyes watched Scott with disturbing, unblinking intensity.

Scott forced himself to go on. "We need men—fighting men—to protect the church while it's being rebuilt. You have those men. You told me so yourself. With some of your men acting as guards and backing me up, Talbot wouldn't try anything else against the church."

He thought her lips curled ever so briefly in a sneer. "Maybe you don't know Land Talbot," she said.

"I know him."

She looked down into the amber liquid in her glass. "What makes you think I'd be willing to help you or your preacher?"

"To help the town. If brawls and gunfights are bad for Meridian, then burning a church and shooting down the preacher can't help it any."

She drained her glass more slowly this time. She turned to the bar so that he could not see her face as she poured. "It could be different between us," she said. "I still have a place for you."

Scott shook his head slowly, although he knew she couldn't see the motion. "It wouldn't be the right place."

She turned back sharply toward him. Scott saw Lobo go rigid. "I gave you my offer of help. Ten thousand dollars for that sorry piece of land. You and your preacher turned it down. I even warned you, but you wouldn't listen. Don't come whining around here now that you've suffered the consequences." She held herself fiercely erect.

"That's your last word?"

"Yes. Now get out."

Scott had the impression of something brittle in her that might shatter at any moment. "Good-bye, Belle," he said, and let himself out.

Chapter Nine

"Everything went so well at the church service yesterday," Ruth said happily over breakfast. "Maybe Talbot's given up. Maybe he'll leave us alone from now on."

Her good cheer, as usual, was catching, Scott mused. Indeed, yesterday's hymn service would have been the perfect opportunity for Talbot to renew hostilities. But things had gone without a hitch. Scott remembered the blending of the untrained voices into a harmonious whole. "At any rate, he'll probably wait a while before trying anything else," he agreed aloud.

His analysis was an accurate one, he told himself. The time for Talbot to have struck was yesterday. Scott, Matt, Seth, and some of the other farmers had rotated turns as lookouts during the service. Nothing had disturbed them. After the brutal shooting of Sam and the burning of the church, Talbot was probably content to lie low for the time being. And perhaps Ruth was right. Faced with the stubborn determination of the Prentiss family not to be moved, Talbot might have decided to cut his losses. He had been an alarmist to go to Belle for help when none was really needed, Scott thought.

"I'll go into town and see about buying some more lumber," Scott said.

"I'll start to clear the building site," Matt volunteered.

Scott nodded approval. "I won't be gone long. Keep your rifle handy." It should be safe to leave the pair of them here alone with their recuperating father, he calculated.

"I need to take this oatmeal to Father." Ruth rose and carried the steaming bowl to the tent.

Brother Sam was doing well, Scott reflected as he saddled the sorrel. The pastor seemed to have actually drawn physical strength from the hymn service the day before. Ruth had had to admonish him more than once not to risk reopening his wound by singing with such vigor from where he sat propped up in the back of the wagon during the service.

Riding into town, Scott smiled at Brother Sam's enthusiasm. Not too much time would pass, he felt certain, before the preacher was up and about. He'd probably run the rest of them ragged supervising the building project.

It took Scott nearly an hour to find a lumber dealer willing to do business with him. He didn't bother to try the general store. Lumber was hard to come by with the building boom in this plains region, and credit was almost as difficult to acquire.

His deal made, he put the sorrel into a lope toward camp. He needed to hitch the wagon and get back to town to pick up the lumber before the grumpy dealer could change his mind.

As he rode into camp he became aware of Matt sitting stiffly on the seat of the wagon. The stricken look on the youth's face made Scott pull the sorrel up short. "What is it?" he demanded. "What's wrong?"

Before Matt could reply, a huge, familiar figure stepped into view from behind the wagon. The bearded giant whom Scott had fought on his first day in town was grinning. He held a gun. It looked like a child's toy in his big fist, but it was pointed competently enough up at Matt.

"They took Ruth," Matt stammered. "They came in and got her and rode out. I couldn't reach my rifle in time. I'm sorry."

The horror of his miscalculation struck Scott with numbing force. Talbot had not been content to lie low. He had not given up or cut his losses. He had struck again while Scott had left the camp virtually defenseless. A hard fist and a loaded gun.

"Your pa?" Scott asked tightly.

Matt swallowed hard. "He's okay. He's still in the tent."

Scott forced his mind to a cold, calculating stillness. He shifted his gaze to the grinning gunman. The man's dead drop on Matt made resistance a greenhorn's play. Scott looked back at the youth. "Did they hurt her?"

"Oh, she's all right, pilgrim," the big man spoke up. "And she'll stay that way just as long as you behave and follow orders."

Scott's eyes scanned searchingly over the camp. The big man's horse was tied beneath a cottonwood.

"There's just me," he told Scott. "All the rest are with the girl."

Scott looked at him again. The bearded face still bore the fading marks of their fight. The fellow was enjoying himself, however. Scott thought he might be able to draw his .45 and drop him before he pulled the trigger on Matt. He kept his hand clear of his gun. The risk was too great. "What orders?" he asked.

The big man disregarded the question. "You know, Colton, me and the boys couldn't believe it when we heard you were talking about rebuilding the church. Heck, everybody knows you ain't no preacher." His chuckle was a sadistic rumble. "Mr. Talbot couldn't believe it, either. It took him a while to decide what to do about it. He decided just killing the preacher was too easy, seeing as how you all had put us to such trouble. He wanted you and the preacher to sweat a little bit."

Scott *was* sweating. He waited for the big man to continue.

"Mr. Talbot set some of us to watching the camp while he decided what to do. We heard all that pretty singing yesterday." His sneer was scornful. "Mr. Talbot finally figured what we should do. Then, when you went riding into town all by your lonesome, just big as life, it gave us the chance we needed."

He had been a fool, Scott realized bitterly. But self-recriminations would not help now. "What does Talbot want?"

"Your tail nailed to a wall, Colton." The little eyes buried in the battered face glittered wickedly. "But he figures your sweating this out is almost as good, maybe better. He wants for all of you to be gone. You and the preacher and the kid here pack your things and pull out. That's Mr. Talbot's orders for you."

"What then?" Scott stilled the sorrel's restless movement.

"Well, the three of you head into Guthrie and get on the first train to Oklahoma City. We'll see that the pastor's pretty little daughter meets you in Oklahoma City safe and sound. Of course, if it was me making plans for that cute little filly. . . ." His words trailed off lasciviously.

Scott didn't waste time on threats. At the moment, they would have all been empty. "How will we get word to Talbot that we're following orders?"

The big man read Scott's capitulation into the question. "Oh, he'll know," he boasted gleefully.

Slowly Scott dismounted. He was careful to make no fast movements and to keep his hands in sight. On the ground, he confronted the bigger man. The giant was watching him, but he kept his gun centered on Matt's vulnerable form.

"You finished with what you got to say now?" Scott asked.

The big man nodded. "That's why Mr. Talbot left me here, to make sure you got the message straight. He says you ain't ever to come back to these parts or he won't be such a gentleman next time. Ha!"

"Anything else?"

"Yeah. He says if you come after him, the girl dies, and it won't be pretty. He also said to tell you that he's pulled his men out of this area except for me. So don't go looking for them with any ideas of getting even by taking them out."

"What's your name?"

The big man hesitated in surprise. "Shep Howard."

"Well, you've delivered your message, Shep." Scott was aware of Matt staring down at both of them from the wagon seat. He wondered what the youth had made of his performance.

Shep took two steps backward toward his horse. He grinned sneeringly and holstered his gun. "I'll be seeing you, pilgrim." He started to turn away.

"You don't think I'm going to let you ride out of here all by your lonesome, just big as life, do you?" Scott asked mockingly. He drew the .45 lazily.

Shep paused and glanced back at him. "It won't do you no good to kill me," he said with assurance. "And it might get your little girlie hurt some." He started once more toward his horse.

"Take another step and I'll blow your foot off."

The big man locked himself rigid in midstride. His bearded head came slowly around to stare. He had gone pale beneath his bruises.

"Turn around," Scott ordered.

Shep shuffled around to face him.

"Take your gun out careful and drop it. Then raise your hands."

Shep complied. Rage and fear twitched his mouth spastically. "This won't do you no good," he protested. "Mr. Talbot won't do a deal with you over me. He won't swap that girl for me. You'll just get her killed. I ain't worth anything to Mr. Talbot."

"You ain't worth anything to anybody," Scott told

him coldly. "Except maybe to that preacher in there who you gunned down. He's probably worried about your soul. I'm not."

"It wasn't me that shot him!" Shep blurted. "It was Strike Foster."

"Thanks. I was wondering about that."

Shep brightened hopefully. "Then you'll let me go?"

"Don't be stupid. Matt, get some rope."

"You'll just get that little girl hurt, Colton!" Shep cried.

"Talbot won't hurt her on your account, Shep. Like you said, you're worthless to him."

Wide-eyed, Matt brought the rope. When he was satisfied with the tie job, Scott left Shep lying bound and helpless in the dirt. He started toward the tent.

Matt caught up with him. "I didn't know what you were going to do," he said breathlessly.

"I didn't intend to let him go." Scott kept walking.

"Do you think Talbot will trade Ruth for him?"

Scott paused. They were out of Shep's earshot. "We might be able to use him as a bargaining chip at some point, although I doubt it. He's not worth enough to Talbot."

"Then why'd you take him prisoner?"

"Because it makes one less of Talbot's men we'll have to go up against."

Matt gaped at him. "You mean we're going after them?"

Scott nodded. "This is one of those times you have to fight. We don't have any guarantee that Talbot will keep his word even if we cut and run like he wants us to. In fact, I'd say the chances are that he won't let

Ruth go unharmed. He's got too big a hate on against me and your father. We don't have any choice on this one. When they take one of your own, it's self-defense."

"I agree," said a labored voice from the mouth of the tent. Brother Sam leaned on a rifle as a makeshift crutch just within the tent. His sweating face was drawn tight with the pain of his exertions. "You've got to go get her," he continued. He swayed alarmingly.

Scott and Matt caught him as his strength failed him. He collapsed into their arms. "Don't worry about me," he gasped. "Go after them. I'll be all right."

Together they helped him back to bed. Matt's anguished gaze over his father's shoulder told Scott what he already knew. They could not leave Brother Sam unattended while they went after Talbot. He needed care. And he needed a place where he would be safe from possible retaliation by Talbot. Through the open flap of the tent, Scott could see the struggling and bound shape of Shep Howard. The big gunman was another problem.

"Stay with your pa for a minute," Scott told Matt.

He didn't wait for an answer, but turned and left the tent. Images of Ruth in the hands of Talbot and the likes of Shep Howard burned in his mind. He tried to force them away. He stared at Shep Howard. He thought hard, and suddenly he had the answers.

He ducked back into the tent. "Get your pa ready to travel," he said crisply. "We're calling in a man's marker, and we're taking another man up on an offer."

They placed Brother Sam in the bed of the wagon despite his protests that they not waste time with his needs. Scott got Shep Howard mounted on the big

man's own horse. Howard's protests were of a decid-
edly different nature than those of the pastor. Scott ignored his curses and bound his ankles beneath the belly
of his horse. Scott kept his Winchester across his saddle
as they moved out.

Seth Brown saw their small caravan coming. The taciturn farmer had trudged in from the field with his oldest son and stood awaiting them as they halted in front
of his sod house. He listened silently as Scott related
what had happened. Seth's knowing gaze shifted to the
mounted Shep. He fingered his carbine suggestively.

"I'll round up some of the other farmers and we'll
go with you," he announced grimly when Scott finished.

Scott could envision what would happen if Seth and
other farmers, willing though they might be, went up
against Land Talbot and his professional gunmen. He
did not want that kind of massacre on his conscience.
"No," he said, "it's better if Matt and I do this alone.
Ruth is his sister and I've done this sort of thing before.
We can move in under cover where a larger party of
men couldn't." He went on before Seth could challenge
his analysis. "What we need is a place to leave Shep
where he isn't likely to be found if Talbot comes looking, and where he can't escape."

He was still asking Seth to run a risk, Scott reflected,
but it was not as great a one as matching his carbine
against professional fighting men.

"We'll throw him in the cellar," Seth said without
hesitation. "He won't get away and he won't be found.
If he tries anything, it'd pleasure me to shoot him dead,

him and any others of his kind who'd steal a young girl like that Ruth."

"Colton, you ain't going to leave me with him?" Howard pleaded.

Scott ignored him. "We'll come back for him," he told Seth. "If we don't, you can turn him over to the law in Guthrie."

Seth nodded. "What about the pastor?" he inquired. "We can put him up too. Janey can look after him."

Scott shook his head. Brother Sam was a lightning rod. Scott couldn't ask this God-fearing farmer to run the risk to himself and his family that sheltering Sam might entail. "I've got somewhere else where he'll be safe."

They bundled the cursing Howard into the gloom of the storm cellar. Seth snapped a padlock through the hasp. "That'll hold him," he said.

Matt looked questioningly at Scott. "Won't we need him to tell us where they're holding Ruth?"

"We couldn't trust him," Scott answered. "And we don't need him. Finding Ruth won't be hard. I used to make my living tracking men like Land Talbot."

Scott spotted the scouts before they reached the Indian village. He detected silent figures kneeling in the tall grass on surrounding hills at the four points of the compass. Hunting Wolf was taking the potential danger seriously, he was relieved to see. He doubted that Talbot would again be able to attack the village by surprise.

He glanced back at the wagon. Matt handled the team, and Shep Howard's big chestnut gelding trotted behind at the end of a lead. Brother Sam seemed to have stood up well to the rigors of the trip. He managed a tight-lipped nod of encouragement as he met Scott's glance. Scott urged the sorrel down toward the village.

A small crowd gathered to meet them. Scott spotted the pretty face of Running Doe. Hunting Wolf came shouldering through the ranks. His dark features clouded even darker as he took in Brother Sam's supine form. He greeted Scott and Matt gravely.

"The white man Talbot has done this," he said.

Scott told him what had happened. Hunting Wolf's black eyes were like chips of onyx as he listened.

"I need a safe place to leave the pastor," Scott finished. "A place where Talbot and his men can't get to him even if they learn of his presence."

"He stay here," Hunting Wolf stated without discussion. "My people not forget how you and your pastor help us defend our homes. Now we help you."

"There could be danger for your people if my plans don't work out," Scott warned.

"There already danger for my people. This way maybe help stop danger."

"We'll be back for him as soon as we can." Both he and Hunting Wolf recognized the real possibility that they might not survive to come back for the pastor, Scott realized.

"We take care of him." Hunting Wolf looked about him at his village. His brow furrowed as his gaze returned to Scott. "Not good that my people ride with you to fight Talbot. Other white men only say my people go to war again, and then they send troops. But I go with you, Scott Colton. I ride to help bring back your woman. My father teach me the old ways to hunt and to kill. I not forget them."

Scott looked in the brave's eyes and knew he could not refuse. This was Hunting Wolf's fight as well as that of his people. The Prentiss family and the Indians shared a common enemy. "All right," he agreed.

Brother Sam was lodged in one of the frame buildings. Running Doe promised to see to his care.

"I'll be praying for you," Brother Sam told Scott from the pallet where he had been placed.

Scott found comfort in the words. He nodded without answering, and left the pastor to the ministrations of the young Indian woman.

Outside, Hunting Wolf was cautioning the people of the village to be on guard. One of the other braves brought him a stocky black and white paint horse little larger than a pony. The animal looked tough and wiry.

Hunting Wolf sprang astride. He carried his bow and arrows slung across his back along with an old Winchester. A hand ax and a bowie knife hung in sheaths at his waist.

Matt swung up onto Shep Howard's chestnut. He carried the gunman's big revolver in the belt of his pants. A rifle was in its boot on the saddle. His face was determined.

Scott had his own old .44 Colt Dragoon in his gun belt. His .45 was holstered. The extra firepower might be helpful. He surveyed his small army and offered up a prayer that they would be in time.

"Let's move," he said.

Chapter Ten

They cut the trail due east of the Indian village. Talbot and his men, presumably with their captive, were headed northeast. Scott had noted the direction of the outlaws' departure from the Prentiss family camp. He had led Matt and Hunting Wolf eastward from the Indian village on the assumption that Talbot had not changed direction and that they could intercept his trail. His calculations had been correct, he realized with relief.

Hunting Wolf had grunted when he realized the direction the outlaws were headed, but he offered no further comment.

The trail was easy to follow. Talbot was making no effort to conceal it. Apparently he felt confident of the power that his possession of Ruth gave him over his adversaries.

Matt had counted nine men in the raid, including Talbot and Foster. Was that all of Talbot's men? Counting Shep Howard and the man Scott had

155

wounded at their first encounter, Talbot had at least seven men out of action. He would have no more than ten men left at the most, Scott guessed. High odds for a gunman, a preacher's kid, and an Indian brave.

The trail did not veer from the northeasterly course as the afternoon lengthened. Urgency hammered at Scott, but he knew better than to rush blindly into what might be a trap. He kept a wary eye on the surrounding terrain.

Hunting Wolf, in the lead, reined up. "I know where they go," he stated.

"Where?" Scott asked quickly.

"They have canyon some miles ahead." Hunting Wolf gestured in the direction they traveled. "My people know these white men stay there. We avoid canyon. But I certain it where these men go."

"Tell us about it," Scott directed. "Describe it." He remembered that Hunting Wolf had mentioned such a hideout at their first meeting. A canyon was not to be expected in this rolling range country, but he did not challenge the Indian's knowledge of the area.

Hunting Wolf dismounted beside a bare patch of ground. As Scott and Matt joined him, he drew his big-bladed bowie knife and began to sketch in the red dirt. Scott listened as the brave explained his drawing. He asked an occasional question. Hunting Wolf seemed confident of his answers.

Talbot and his men had erected a log cabin and a bunkhouse in a shallow canyon cut by a creek. Woods cloaked the edges of the canyon on both sides. The tapering end of the canyon and both sloping sides were protected by numerous barbed-wire fences hung with empty tin cans and bottles to create an alarm should an enemy attempt to penetrate the barrier. The horses were corralled just inside the innermost stretch of barbed wire. Their presence provided a further obstacle to anyone attempting entrance through this route. The wider mouth of the canyon served as the usual entrance for the outlaws. A guard was generally posted on the edge of one of the cliffs overlooking the entrance.

Given the nature of the local terrain, it was about as good a spot as Talbot could want, Scott reflected. And he appeared to have done a passable job of securing it from invasion. With Ruth in his possession, Talbot would most likely double the guard at the canyon mouth, Scott guessed. He would also be likely to have at least one man posted on the canyon floor near wherever Ruth was imprisoned.

Talbot usually occupied the log cabin, according to Hunting Wolf. It was there, the warrior believed, that Ruth would be held. Scott felt his gorge rise at the thought, but forced himself to concentrate on Hunting Wolf's sketch.

"How long until we reach there?" he asked.

Hunting Wolf looked to the east. The orange ball of the sun was well down toward the horizon. "We not reach there until after dark," he predicted.

Scott frowned. Night was probably the best time to launch an attack, but he would have liked to see the layout by daylight. He shook his head impatiently. It could not be helped, and their time was limited. Talbot would soon be wondering at the absence of Shep Howard. They could not afford to wait for daylight. At least the darkness would provide cover for disposing of the sentries.

Scott spoke, formulating his plan even as he described it. His companions listened silently. Once or twice Hunting Wolf grunted.

"Good plan," he said when Scott was finished.

Scott looked at Matt. "Can you handle your part of it?" he questioned. "A lot will be riding on you."

Matt nodded. "I can do it."

"Good man." Scott looked to Hunting Wolf, who nodded his assent to the plan. They remounted and rode out.

Dusk was fast gathering when they came to an extensive stand of woodland. Scott guessed that a creek must wind through the area, thereby creating the heavier plant growth and permitting the formation of the small canyon.

They left their horses tied and went forward on foot. They moved with caution. Scott was an old hand at this type of silent travel, and Hunting Wolf had been tutored by masters. He passed through the darkness like a wraith. Matt followed closely behind Scott. The youth made surprisingly little noise, considering his inexperience.

After a quarter mile Hunting Wolf motioned them to halt. They had reached the edge of the canyon, which was really more of an enormous gully, Scott thought. The sides, for the most part, were not particularly steep. The light of the rising moon glinted off the wicked points of the barbed wire strung in staggered rows down the slopes. The dangling cans and bottles swayed slightly in the evening breeze. Wind would give rise to false alarms by clattering some of the cans and bottles together, Scott figured. It was a formidable defense for the outlaws' enclave.

A large bonfire had been lit to illuminate the canyon floor. The cabin and the bunkhouse were easily discernible. There was also a smaller structure, which Scott took to be a storage shed. Several men were visible, moving leisurely about the canyon floor or visiting with one another. Scott spotted two of them prowling purposefully near the cabin. Two guards instead of the one he had expected, he thought grimly. Talbot was being cautious. But the guards' presence meant that Ruth was almost certainly in the cabin.

He had seen enough, and he motioned his companions to withdraw. Back with the horses, they held a whispered conference. Scott had not seen anything to dissuade him from implementing his plan.

"Stay with the horses," he instructed Matt. "Keep them quiet. We'll be back. Don't let anybody come up on you from behind."

Matt nodded. He held his Winchester firmly and did not seem overly nervous or afraid. Scott felt better about bringing the youth into this. But he had really not had any choice.

Scott took time to find a sturdy club. Its length made it preferable to a rock for the work that lay ahead. In a pinch he could use the .45 or the Dragoon, but guns were too easily damaged for use in this kind of work.

He saw Hunting Wolf draw his bowie and plunge it into the soil. The dirt dulled the gleam of the big blade. Hunting Wolf tested its edge with a practiced thumb. The deadly blade would see use this night, Scott thought. He had used a knife himself on more than one occasion. He would stick to his club or a rock.

Hunting Wolf's face was enigmatic in the gloom. The brave nodded his readiness, and Scott motioned him to lead off. Hunting Wolf knew the terrain and probable sites of the guards. As the brush closed about them, Scott's senses felt attuned to some dark level of the night. Ahead of him, Hunting Wolf was a dim and predatory figure.

He was a predator too, Scott realized—a manhunter once again. Only this time there was a difference. The bounty on his prey was the life and love of a good and virtuous woman. He had never stalked a quarry so dangerous or gambled for a stake so high.

He guessed they must be nearing the mouth of the canyon. The shadow that was Hunting Wolf came to a silent halt. Wordlessly the brave pointed. It took Scott a moment to discern the upright figure leaning against an outcropping of rock. Here was one of Talbot's guards, positioned to command a view of much of the canyon below. If Scott's calculations were correct, there would be another guard stationed on the opposite side of the canyon's mouth.

Scott nodded so that Hunting Wolf would know he had his prey spotted. Hunting Wolf pointed to the moon visible through the branches overhead. Then he moved his finger to a point higher and farther west in the night sky. Again Scott indicated his understanding. When the moon had reached that place in the sky, Hunting Wolf would be in position on the far side of the canyon mouth. Better, they had agreed, that both guards be taken out simultaneously so as to avoid the possibility of one of them alerting the other with an out-cry. Of course, if things went as planned, there would be no outcries.

Hunting Wolf disappeared into the dappled gloom. Scott settled down silently to wait. He tried to keep watch on his prey without staring directly at him or even concentrating on him. More than one potential victim, Scott included, had been alerted by feeling the gaze of a waiting enemy.

The fellow was some ten yards distant. The rock out-cropping against which he leaned towered above his head. It would be impossible to approach him from the rear. Scott's attack would have to be from the side or front. Scott preferred the side.

He fingered his club as he crouched in the darkness. The makeshift weapon was a piece of dead, weathered branch. It had about the length and heft of an ax han-dle. Scott hoped it would do the job.

The moon edged across the sky. It diminished in di-ameter and brightness as it ascended. Scott thought of Hunting Wolf slipping stealthily through the trees, knife in hand. He gripped his club tighter. It was almost time.

The guard had not stirred other than to straighten and stretch a couple of times. A rifle leaned against the rocks beside him. He seemed competent and alert. He had not even lit a cigarette, which could betray his posi-tion to a watcher. He might not be easy to take.

It was time, and Scott began to edge closer. Once started, his attack would have to be carried home swiftly and decisively. He could not afford a prolonged struggle.

As the guard looked in his direction, Scott felt sure that his eyes passed over him. But the man did not discern his crouching form. As his prey's head turned back toward the canyon, Scott went for him in a rush.

There was no way to be silent. Scott saw the guard spin toward the sound of his rush. He glimpsed a face, pale and startled in the darkness. The man reached for his gun as Scott swung the club. He felt the club smash against the side of his prey's neck. The impact vibrated up through Scott's arms. The guard was driven sideways against the rock. Reflexively his hand lifted his gun. Scott dropped the club and shot his left hand down to clamp about the rising revolver. He felt the cylinder start to turn against his palm, pinching his flesh. His grip halted the turn of the cylinder. The guard slumped. The gun came free in Scott's hand. Only reflex had let the guard cock it and try to pull the trigger. Even unconscious, he had almost succeeded in alerting the camp.

Scott checked his victim's pulse and could feel the blood still pumping beneath the skin. Good, his prey still lived. Swiftly he stripped the fellow's shirt from him and used it to bind and gag him. Satisfied, he collected the revolver and the rifle still leaning against the rock outcropping. They would be too cumbersome for him to carry into battle in addition to his other arms, but Matt might well have use for them.

Once more he waited. There had been no disturbance from across the canyon. Hunting Wolf must likewise have succeeded in his deadly task.

The canyon spread out below Scott in dim relief. There was not much activity now. The fire had burned low. Most of the men must have retired to the bunkhouse. The two guards still prowled near the cabin. Scott tried to banish from his mind the cruel images of what might be transpiring behind those log walls. Mentally he urged Hunting Wolf to hurry.

Then the brave was there. He seemed to take substance out of the darkness. He gave a barely perceptible grunt of acknowledgment. Together they headed back toward where Matt waited with the horses. As they drew near, Scott called out softly to alert the youth. Matt was waiting vigilantly when they reached him. He was fingering the lever action of his Winchester.

Scott discarded his club for his own Winchester. Hurrying some, they returned to the canyon's edge. He selected a site commanding a good view of the cabin and bunkhouse. A jumble of boulders offered concealment and a rifle rest. Scott gave the captured handgun and rifle to Matt and repeated his earlier instructions in a terse whisper. Matt nodded grimly in response. They left him there kneeling among the boulders, his firearms at hand.

Scott and Hunting Wolf moved quickly along the canyon's rim just within the cover of the trees. Scott did not know when or if the guards might be replaced, but they could not risk taking much longer than they already had. Like ghosts, they slipped around through the unguarded mouth onto the floor of the canyon.

The dying fire cast little light. Still, they stayed to the deeper shadows at the base of the canyon wall. Somewhere above them Matt would be watching and waiting. Had he detected their presence? Scott hoped that the youth would not freeze when the time for action came.

In front of them, past the bunkhouse, he could see the nearer of the two guards. The other one must be out of sight behind the cabin. No other men were visible. A light shone from the window of the bunkhouse.

Scott paused to indicate the nearer guard, and then pointed at Hunting Wolf. The bowie appeared in the warrior's hand. His rifle was slung across his shoulders by a tattered rope.

Scott left him behind and skulked swiftly through the shadows at the base of the cliff. Once past the cabin, he spotted the figure of the other guard. The man was sauntering lazily across the floor of the canyon. His back was to Scott. The glow of a cigarette silhouetted his head. This one was not as careful as the man Scott had dispatched above. But here in the hideout itself, he probably believed he had little to fear.

He was wrong, Scott thought grimly.

They were out of sight of the front guard. Hunting Wolf would handle that one. Scott darted across the intervening space. He flattened himself against the side of the cabin. His heart slammed back and forth inside his rib cage. The brassy taste of fear sucked the moisture from his mouth.

He lifted the butt of the Winchester back even with his shoulder. Its barrel angled skyward. It wouldn't do the rifle any good to be used as a club, but he had not wanted to hamper himself with both it and the club now. The rifle would have to serve.

He heard the guard's approach and his muscles went rigid. The guard ambled past ten feet distant. Scott took three swift steps in his wake. He slammed the butt of the Winchester down on the nape of the man's neck. The guard collapsed. One-handed, Scott dragged him into the shadow of the cabin. He did not bother to check this one. Alive or dead, the fellow would be of no further consequence to this night's action.

Scott sprinted away from the cabin toward the fire. Hunting Wolf arose from the darkness to meet him. There was no sign of the guard he had stalked. Scott bent close to the fire, snatched a smoldering brand, and swished it through the air. The rush of air aroused the flames to life. Across the fire, Scott saw Hunting Wolf had similarly armed himself.

Scott ran for the rear of the bunkhouse. Constructed of old dry boards, it was little more than an elongated shack. Overhand he cast the flaming brand onto the structure's roof. He saw the flicker of the flames from in front of the bunkhouse. Hunting Wolf had also thrown his torch onto the roof. Scott stepped back for a better view. He exhaled with grim satisfaction. The dry wood was already beginning to catch.

"Hey! What are you doing?"

Scott levered the Winchester as he turned. He glimpsed the figures of two men already pulling their guns. He had no idea where they had come from. Perhaps they were additional guards set to patrol the canyon floor at random. It didn't matter. Scott triggered the Winchester from waist height. He levered it as he swung the barrel and then fired again. Both men staggered back. One of their guns discharged into the dirt. Scott fired once more at each of them as they fell.

Shouts erupted from within the bunkhouse. The factor of surprise had been lost. Overhead, the flames began to lick toward the night sky.

Scott ran for the cabin. Behind him he heard more yells. Shots sounded at his back and from up on the canyon rim. That would be Hunting Wolf and Matt. According to plan, they were firing on the outlaws as they emerged from the burning bunkhouse. He hoped Hunting Wolf had had time to get into some position clear of the building's front.

Scott heard pistol shots. At least some of the outlaws were returning fire. From the number of shots and the volume of the yells, Scott guessed with despair that he had badly underestimated the amount of men Talbot had at his command. He could not turn back to assist. His target was the cabin.

Gunfire stabbed a roaring lance of flame at him from his right. Hitting the ground on his chest, he twisted desperately onto his side to bring his rifle to bear. From thirty feet he saw his attacker taking careful aim at him with a handgun. The man's first shot had been hasty. His second would not be.

Scott triggered the Winchester twice, levering it as fast as he could. The gunman gave a little jump up and back, then crumpled. Scott scrambled to his feet and ran on. Dimly he realized he had lost the Dragoon revolver in his desperate dive to the ground. He was left with only his .45 and his Winchester.

The fire was adding its roar to the cracking of gunfire. The cabin was in front of him and the door was opening. He froze himself in midstep as he saw the figures illuminated by the leaping flames at his back. Strike Foster came stalking into the infernal glare like some great predatory feline. His gun was holstered. He gripped the curved shape of his boomerang in his fist.

Behind Foster were two figures that seemed merged into one. Ruth's face was pale but defiant. Her hands were bound in front of her. A leather thong of some sort encircled her neck. Its end was held by Land Talbot, who loomed tall and ominous at her back. The flames glinted from the barrels of the sawed-off, double-barrel Fox shotgun he held in his other hand. Its barrels were pressed against Ruth's jaw and the side of her neck. Her head was bent slightly sideways from their pressure.

"Talbot!" Scott yelled. There was no way he could fire on the outlaw chieftain without endangering Ruth.

Talbot's head snapped toward him. The shifting glare of the flames made his handsome face satanic. Foster saw Scott too. The gunfighter did not go for his gun. Scott held the Winchester leveled uncertainly in their direction.

"Drop the rifle, Colton, or I blast her head off!" Talbot bawled. "You know this shotgun will do it! My finger's on the triggers!"

The heat of the flames seemed to lick at Scott's back. Over Ruth's shoulder, Talbot's face had become that of a demon. He jerked the thong he held so that Ruth staggered. Her face twisted in pain.

Reluctantly Scott dropped the Winchester to the ground. Talbot's harsh laughter echoed.

"You're mine!" Strike Foster's voice cut through the diminishing echoes. The gunfighter appeared to glide sideways until he was clear of his boss and their hostage. His pale features seemed as white as bleached bone. His grin might have been that of a skull's. "I've waited for this, Colton!" he shouted. With no more warning, his arm lashed forward. The black shape of the boomerang slashed cartwheeling at Scott's head.

Scott leaned aside. He felt the whipping of wind as the whirling club whistled past his face. It had been ridiculously easy to dodge, a remote segment of his mind registered with surprise. He wondered at Foster's reliance on the obscure weapon. Foster's grin grew wider.

The snap of the object's whirling passage through the air from behind warned Scott on some elemental level. He ducked. The boomerang, spinning on a flat axis now, clipped his Stetson from his head in passing. He stared in bewildered shock. Foster plucked the returning weapon from the air with casual ease.

Foster didn't hesitate. His arm flashed back and then forward in a practiced continuation of his catch. The boomerang sprang from his fist again. Scott's gun cleared leather in a fragment of a heartbeat. He fired upward out of instinct and reflex and training. In midair the boomerang splintered into fragments.

As the splinters fell, Foster cried out and made his draw. His gun came up as fast as Scott's. But Scott's .45 was already drawn. He fired twice, thumbing the hammer and pulling the trigger so fast that the two shots merged into one. Foster took a pace backward and fell to his knees. He made a clumsy, ridiculous motion with his arm, as if he would hurl his gun at Scott as he had hurled the boomerang. He didn't complete it, and fell forward on his face.

Scott swung the .45 to bear on Talbot and his hostage.

"Don't, Colton!" Talbot's voice had grown more shrill. He jammed the barrels of the Fox harder against Ruth's flesh.

"Scott!" she cried. Her voice died to a strangle as Talbot yanked on the noose.

"All this for a lousy church, Colton?" Talbot screamed into the night. "What the devil is it to you?"

Scott was dimly aware of the sporadic gunfire mingling with the crackle of flames to his rear. Talbot shook his head in baffled frustration. Scott wondered that he had ever thought the man handsome. Evil rage had made Talbot's face a horrifying visage and robbed it of any last vestige of handsomeness.

"You've ruined it all!" Talbot cried.

"Good," Scott said coldly. He still could not risk a shot.

"I'm going out of here with her, Colton! Do you hear me?"

Scott didn't answer.

Then Talbot laughed wildly. "But I'll kill you first!" He flipped the barrels of the shotgun down so they rested on Ruth's shoulder, leveled directly at Scott. Ruth cried out in wordless protest. She flung her pinioned hands up against the twin barrels. They were knocked upward and the shotgun blasted toward the stars.

Scott hurled himself forward. He still could not fire. He dropped the .45 as he lunged. He slammed into both of them. He heard the air driven from Ruth's lungs. The shotgun flew from Talbot's hands. They went over backward with Ruth sandwiched between them. Then she kicked and thrust herself clear, rolling free of them.

Scott had an instant to snatch Talbot's handgun from its holster and hurl it away.

Then Talbot's legs locked around his middle like a vise. Hard thumbs gouged up at his eyes. Talbot was big and strong, and somewhere along the line he had been schooled in the deadly techniques of a particularly nasty form of grappling combat.

Scott ducked away from the gouging thumbs. The thick thumbnails raked his forehead. Talbot's clamped thighs locked him immobile in their scissors grip. Talbot snarled savagely up at him. The outlaw tried to interlace his fingers behind Scott's head and drive his thumbs home again.

Desperately Scott raised his fists and hammered their edges down to Talbot's chest. Talbot grunted. Scott ducked clear of his groping hands. Talbot's legs were still around him, and he felt his chest and middle being constricted by their cruel pressure.

Scott gasped for air. He got his knees under him. With an effort that strained every muscle in his body, he rose trembling to his feet. Anchored to Scott's body by the leg scissors, Talbot was lifted clear of the ground. Scott fell on him. Talbot smashed to the ground on his back with Scott's weight behind the fall. As they fell, Scott rammed both fists down into Talbot's chest again.

Talbot's legs loosened. Scott wrestled himself free. He tried to dodge clear. Talbot clamped his legs about Scott's leg and twisted it from under him. Scott fell hard, and he scrabbled to regain his feet before Talbot could. He succeeded, and hooked a right to Talbot's rising jaw that twisted his head around.

Talbot grabbed for Scott's right arm with cruelly

practiced hands. Scott felt his arm bent and twisted in
a punishing lock. The pain would have paralyzed him
had he let it. In another instant the pressure would dis-
locate his arm. Scott swung his left fist at Talbot's ear.
Cartilage crumpled beneath his knuckles. Talbot
grunted in pain. His grip weakened. Scott swung again.

Talbot twisted past him. The bigger man's powerful
arms clamped about his throat from behind. Scott's air
was cut off abruptly. Redness began to tinge his vision.
Dimly he was aware of Talbot's panting breath in his
ears. His repeated blows to Talbot's chest had hurt the
outlaw and interfered with his breathing. He drove an
elbow backward. It caught Talbot's ribs. Talbot gasped.
Scott hooked his foot back behind Talbot's ankle. He
kicked out sharply and flung his weight back hard
against his captor. Talbot's leg was yanked out from
under him. They crashed backward to the ground, Talbot on the bottom. Scott's full weight landed atop his
chest. Talbot's stranglehold fell away. Talbot wasn't the
only one who knew some wrestling tricks, Scott
thought with savage exultation.

He rolled off Talbot and pushed himself up to his
feet. Talbot came lurching erect. Half doubled in pain
from his battered chest, he lunged for Scott's throat
with taloned hands. His fingers dug painfully into flesh
and nerve and muscle. Even weakened, his grip was ter-
rible.

Scott set his feet and whipped right and left into Talbot's rib cage with all his strength. Talbot's mouth
snapped open wide in anguish. He whined. His fingers
peeled away from Scott's throat. He staggered back a
pace. Scott stepped after him and hit him hard in the

middle. Talbot wrapped his arms around his battered torso and fell to his knees. He tried but was unable to rise. Gasping, panting, barely able to draw air into his tortured lungs, he stared up at Scott.

Scott swayed. His own breathing was none too easy. His neck felt as though it had almost been wrung.

Talbot tried once more to rise, then sank back in defeat. "Blast you, Colton!" he rasped. "You shouldn't have beaten us. All the odds were against you."

"You told me yourself once that maybe the odds weren't as high as you thought," Scott said. He stepped in and swung again. It was a looping downward blow to the jaw. It toppled Talbot senselessly over onto his side.

Scott turned as Ruth rushed over to him. Her hands were still bound in front of her. "Thank the Lord!" she gasped breathlessly. "I prayed so hard. . . ."

Scott fumbled ineffectually at the knots on her wrists. Then a heavy blade slipped between them and severed the thongs effortlessly. Hunting Wolf gave them both a rare smile.

Scott looked past the Indian. The bunkhouse still burned. A number of still forms were sprawled in front of it. He realized that the battle had been decided in their favor during his confrontation with Talbot and Foster.

"Men dead or gone," Hunting Wolf confirmed his thoughts. "Boy do good." A jerk of his head indicated Matt's position on the canyon rim.

Their strategy had worked. With Matt on the rim above, and Hunting Wolf on the canyon floor, the outlaws had made ready targets as they fled the burning bunkhouse. Matt would even now be making his way down to the canyon floor.

"That's all of them, then," Scott said.

Hunting Wolf shook his head. "No, not all," he stated solemnly. "My people watch this place. Many times we see one from town come here and stay in cabin with Talbot."

"Who was it?" Ruth asked quickly.

In the moment before Hunting Wolf replied, Scott guessed the answer.

Chapter Eleven

The opulent interior of the Dark Lady was almost empty. The lone morning bartender started to protest as Scott stalked past. He glimpsed Scott's face and kept silent.

Scott pounded at the heavy door under the staircase. After a moment he sensed movement behind it. He was tired and worn by the night's events and the ride that had brought him here. But suddenly he felt a cool alertness.

The door opened. He glimpsed surprise in the black, beguiling eyes. There were dark rings of exhaustion under them. Belle Tanner seemed to have lost the last of her youth. Beneath her robe she wore the same sheer nightgown that Scott had seen her wear before. The sight of her left him cold.

She recovered her poise quickly. "Did you come for another favor?" Her voice carried all the old mockery.

Scott remembered their first meeting and her subtle

174

manipulation of him. "I don't need any more of your favors," he said.

"Come in." She stepped aside to let him enter, then seemed to sway closer toward him as he passed. Scott caught the mingled scents of perfume and whiskey.

Lobo stood at her heels. Like a gray shadow the big wolf dog followed her as she moved to the bar. She leaned back brazenly against its mahogany surface. "Well, if it's not a favor, what is it? Have you reconsidered my offer?" Her smile was lewd. Scott detected a hint of strain beneath it.

"Land Talbot sends his regards," he told her.

Nothing altered in her face. It seemed to freeze into a porcelain mask. "What do you mean?"

"It's all over, Belle. I know who your secret partner is in the Dark Lady and all your other enterprises here in Meridian. I guess he provided the funding for you back when you worked in a place like this."

She stared at him without answering. By her side, Lobo was as immobile as she.

Scott sighed. "We took Ruth away from Talbot. Most of his men are dead. The others are probably almost out of the Territory by now."

She emitted a deep, shuddering breath. "Blast him!" she said almost to herself. "I told him that kidnapping the girl wouldn't work. It was stupid and unnecessary. There were other ways to get rid of you and your preacher and his church. But Land never would listen. He had to make you and the preacher suffer. His answer to everything was to shoot, or to hurt, or to burn, or to kill."

"But you're more subtle, aren't you?" Scott said.

"You and Talbot never have quite agreed on how to handle me. When you saw me whip three of his boys to protect the preacher, you figured I might be trouble. That's why you wanted to hire me. You tried to buy me, and when that didn't work, you tried to seduce me into your camp. All of your playing up to me was an act."

"Was it?"

"I'm interested. What did Talbot think about it? How did he like the idea of his woman coming on to me?"

She shook her head mutely.

"You used your influence to get the storekeeper to cut off Brother Sam's credit. I didn't think that was Talbot's style. And when all else failed, you tried to buy out Brother Sam. I should've seen it sooner. No wonder you turned me down cold when I came to you for help. You even kept Talbot and his men from trying to kill me that day in the street. You really didn't want that kind of violence in Meridian. I'd guess Talbot wasn't too happy about your stepping in that way."

"He never owned me." Bitterness was in her voice, but she gave her head a defiant lift. "I might've been his woman, but no man owns me. You're right, though. He did help me get started. I was just a saloon girl here when he met me. But I wanted more than that. He could see it in me, and he could see that I'd do whatever needed to be done to get what I wanted. He needed a kind of sanctuary, a refuge where he could come and be safe."

"So you gave him one."

"Yes," she said proudly.

"With your power here in town, you could see to it that the law didn't touch him here. He could bring his men into Meridian for recreation between raids without worrying about the law. With your power in town, the threat of him and his men, and the economic boon it was to the town to have him operating out of here, the townspeople who knew or suspected were willing to turn a blind eye. And in return for providing all that to him, you got what you wanted—money and power and luxury."

"He didn't give it to me!" she spat. "Sure he started me with the saloon, but the rest of what I have I built myself."

"With Talbot as your partner, there was no one who would have had the nerve to cross you or turn you down," Scott pointed out.

She glared. "Think what you want, you and your preacher's daughter. Land didn't own me, but he was more of a man than you'll ever be."

Scott glanced toward the rear entrance to her chambers. It would have been easy for Talbot to come here unobserved. Just as it had been easy for her to go to him at his hideout under the guise of business trips. Some of the townspeople must have known or guessed the truth, but the combined pressures to go along with the arrangement had been too great for anyone to oppose.

With her business contacts, Belle could easily have provided Talbot with information concerning potential robbery targets. She would share in the booty as well as benefit from Talbot's men spending their money in her saloon. And word of the lawless character of Meridian would have quickly spread. It was no wonder that the town was a haven for owlhoots and scavengers.

"You were also able to provide him with information about what happened here in town. That's why he always knew what was going on," Scott continued. "But even you resorted to violence at one point, though, I'll admit, it was a more subtle effort than anything Talbot came up with. What did you do? Send Johnny, your loyal and jealous bartender, out to dry-gulch me and Ruth? Is that why he's no longer around? Because I shot him up too badly?" He saw from the cold flame in her eyes that he had hit on the truth. "You're not really so different from Talbot, after all, under all the fancy clothes and airs."

"You can't understand," she said venomously. "Land and I were good together. One day he was going to give up running outside the law and marry me. Then we'd be respectable. Don't look at me like that! It's true! We loved each other!"

Her twisted passions for the man showed on her face. Whatever relationship she and Land Talbot had had, Scott doubted that it could have been love.

"You and me could've had something too," she said. Scott shook his head. "No, Belle."

"No man's ever turned me down before."

"Why the church?" he asked. "What was Brother Sam doing to hurt you?"

"It was what his church could do to this town! You've seen it in other places—I know you have. Once a town gets a church, things start to change. A church brings in decent people, and they want schools for their children, and honest government, and law and order.

We couldn't let that happen. It would've ruined everything."

Scott recalled his own earlier thoughts about how the church and the Prentiss family had changed him. Belle was right. The moralizing and civilizing effect of a church on a wide-open town like Meridian could be great. It was this influence that had played one of the major roles in the slow taming of the West over the last century. In Brother Sam's simple calling to build a church, Belle and Talbot had glimpsed the beginning of the end of their little empire. It was hardly surprising that they had reacted so strongly to the presence of a church in the community.

"Don't you dare stand there and pity me!" She had seen something in Scott's eyes of which he had not been aware. "I don't need any man's pity, least of all yours!"

"It had to end, Belle," Scott said. "If it hadn't been Brother Sam, it would've been some other preacher. Or maybe just some good God-fearing folks deciding they wanted a clean town. One day this Territory will become a state, and then law and order and churches and schools and decent people and their businesses will come in whether you want them or not. There's no way you could finally win. But that doesn't matter, because it's all finished for you now. And I guess you're right. Maybe I do pity you a little. I shouldn't, but that's what hanging around church people will do to you."

"Nothing's finished for me. I still have the Dark Lady. I still own half this town. You can't prove anything about me and Land."

"We've got Talbot," Scott told her tiredly. "Some of the local farmers who aren't under his thumb or yours are holding him for me. Like I told you, he doesn't have a gang left. The preacher's kid and an Indian and I killed them or ran them off. Talbot's willing to talk so that he doesn't have to take all the blame for what's gone on here. Besides, we've got another man of his as a prisoner. He'll talk, too, to save his neck. One of the farmers is on the way to Guthrie right now to get the U.S. deputy marshal in charge there. It really is all finished, Belle."

"Lobo! Kill!" she screamed.

In a snarling paroxysm of fury, Lobo, unleashed at last, erupted at Scott's throat. Scott snapped his gun out and fired. He twisted away from the wolf dog's hurtling bulk. Ivory fangs snapped within an inch of his face. Lobo crashed to the floor and lay still. Scott's shot had caught him square as he sprang. He had died in midleap. Even in death, he had nearly taken Scott down.

Scott stood over him, gun in hand. He shook his head. Belle had been right—Lobo was faster than any man he had ever faced. He looked at Belle.

She began to curse him then. A stream of foul oaths burst from her mouth, twisting her face until it was ugly. At last she fell silent, glaring at him in savage, impotent anger.

"I do pity you," Scott told her. "But I pity this poor dog a whole lot more."

"It will be good to get back behind the pulpit," Brother Sam said. "Lying here, I've had nothing to do but compose sermons. I can hardly wait to try some of them out on the congregation." His grin was engaging, and his eyes held a twinkle. He looked fit and healthy, Scott reflected. He guessed it wouldn't be much longer until the pastor was, indeed, once more behind the pulpit.

"You'll have a roof over your head when you do preach." Scott gestured at the workers visible through the open flap of the tent.

"I lie here and watch them and think that it's a miracle," Brother Sam said.

Scott followed the direction of his gaze. He could see Seth Brown and his oldest son hard at work with Matt on the porch of the new church building. Other farmers and townspeople who had volunteered to help were visible at various tasks. It did seem incredible that the pristine white church could have risen so rapidly where the pile of blackened rubble had stood not too long ago. Brother Sam would not lack for a congregation.

Scott remembered the pleasure and gratitude he had felt when the volunteers had shown up shortly after Land Talbot, Belle Tanner, and Shep Howard had been taken into custody by the U.S. deputy marshal that Seth had brought from Guthrie. Talbot and Belle, he knew, would pay dearly for their despotic and murderous reign over Meridian.

"There's a verse in Proverbs," Brother Sam commented, "that says something to the effect that the good influence of godly citizens causes a city to prosper, but the moral decay of the wicked drives it to destruction. We've seen the latter side of that. Now I think we'll be seeing the former."

A shadow darkened the tent entrance. Ruth smiled

as she saw Scott within the tent. She carried a covered tray that she set on a stool beside her father's bed.

"It's lunchtime," she said.

"Something solid this time, I hope."

"You've been eating almost the same as the rest of us for several days now," Ruth chided.

Janey Brown and some of the other women had been helping her do the cooking for the workers. Scott watched her now as she fussed around her father. She had a lovely joyfulness that gripped his heart tightly.

She left Brother Sam and came to stand close beside Scott. "Now, don't overdo things," she cautioned her patient. She turned to Scott. "I've been meaning to ask you, have you heard from Hunting Wolf?"

Scott shook his head. "I'm sure he's all right," he told her. "It wasn't a good idea to involve him officially with Talbot's capture."

Ruth nodded. "I know."

Following the raid on Talbot's hideout, Hunting Wolf had slipped away to rejoin his people. Scott had made no mention of him to the deputy marshal. "We'll go see him and Running Doe soon," he promised Ruth.

Her smile was radiant.

"That's another thing I want to do," Brother Sam said. "I need to get back out there to the Indian village and see what can be done for them."

Scott drew a deep breath. "You've got at least one other duty to perform first," he said. He felt Ruth's eyes on him.

"What might that be?" Brother Sam asked.

"Well, once we get the church built," Scott said, "I figure we need to have a wedding."

Ruth gasped. Then suddenly she was in his arms, brimming over with tearful laughter. Scott held her tightly, laughing some himself.

"I guess she accepts," Brother Sam said.

Immediately she twisted around to look at him, although she still held onto Scott. "Is it all right, Father?" she asked breathlessly.

"It's a little late to ask," Brother Sam told her. "But you certainly have my blessings. And I can't wait to perform the ceremony."

She gave a delighted little cry, and ran to kiss him on the cheek.

"I guess I'd better hurry and recuperate," Brother Sam commented as she rejoined Scott. The pastor looked at them with love. "You make a fine couple."

Scott put an arm around Ruth's shoulders and hugged her. He felt a surge of satisfaction and of peace and of happiness. He had fought for the right things, and he had won. And he would continue to fight for them, in one way or another, as long as it was necessary. There really was a way to start over, he thought with gratitude. He had found his new beginning.